P9-DNP-805

The Journal of Ben Uchida

Citizen 13559
Mirror Lake Internment Camp

BY BARRY DENENBERG

Scholastic Inc. New York

San Francisco, California
1942

Tuesday, April 21, 1942

My name is Ben Uchida. My number is 13559.

Actually, it's not just my number, it's my whole family's number. We all have to use that number now, except Papa. He's not going with us. He was taken away last week; we leave tomorrow. There's no furniture anymore. Mama had to sell all of it — everything except the stuff we're storing in Mr. Mills's cellar. I'm writing on the floor now.

Keeping this journal is Robbie's idea. He even gave me the notebook. "This is history in the making," he said. That's why I gave him the nickname Motto Man. He thinks all this madness should be recorded and he made me pinky him that I would write everything down, so that's what I'm doing. I don't see what good it's going to do but a promise is a promise — especially when it's your best friend — so I figured I would get down everything that happened up till now.

It all started last year, just a couple of weeks before Christmas. "The Christmas that never was," that's what

Naomi called it. She's my older sister. She's fourteen, same age as Robbie. I'm twelve. I'll be thirteen next January.

It was a Sunday and I was riding my bike back from Robbie's. I was riding real fast because I didn't want to be late again for dinner. We had been playing touch football all day with Larry Light, Tommy La Motta, Frankie Lemon, and some of the other kids. Robbie and me went down to the switching yards after the game so we could lay some pennies on the tracks. That's why I was so late.

On the way home, I had the feeling that people were looking at me, but I didn't pay too much attention to it. But as soon as I walked in the door I knew something was wrong. For one thing, Naomi was crying. Naomi never cries. Never ever. And if that wasn't enough of a clue, the look on Mama's face was.

The radio was turned up real loud, which was unusual because Papa doesn't like that. The announcer was talking so fast I could barely make out what he was saying. Something about "Jap" airplanes and a surprise attack at Pearl Harbor. He said "Japs," not Japanese, so you knew he meant it in a mean way.

I never heard of Pearl Harbor but I figured it must be around here somewhere. That would explain why Naomi was crying. She was scared that the Japanese were coming to bomb San Francisco next. Everyone was listening so closely to the radio that they didn't even look at me when I sat down.

Naomi asked Papa how they could do this but Papa just shook his head and said, "*Nihon baka da ne*," which meant that Papa thought the Japanese had done a foolish thing. No one said anything during dinner. No one ate much either. We were all listening to the man on the radio repeating the same horrible news over and over.

That night I woke up because I could smell smoke. When I got downstairs, I could hear Mama and Papa out in the backyard. They were out where Papa burns the dead leaves and there *was* a fire, but it was December and there were no leaves left to burn. Instead they were throwing newspapers, records, and books into the fire. Even the books Papa read to me when I was little. He was ripping them apart one by one and throwing them in. Mama was taking the rubber bands off the packets of letters from Grandma and Grandpa. The ones that she kept on the top shelf in the hall closet. She hesitated for a moment after she took off each rubber band, then threw them up in the air so they would scatter before they came down on the flames.

I could see that Mama's photo albums and Naomi's Japanese dolls were next. I couldn't believe what I was seeing. I couldn't speak. I stood there watching for a long time, even though I was cold.

They were startled when I did speak. I guess they didn't hear me coming because of the fire, which was fizzing and crackling loudly. Papa was angry. He said I should go back to bed immediately, but I just stood there, shivering. Mama came over, put her arm around my shoulder, and led me inside.

I asked her why they were burning everything. She said that because of what happened at Pearl Harbor, it was dangerous to have any Japanese things around the house now. But that didn't explain why she was burning her pictures of Grandma and Grandpa. Mama said that the pictures were taken a few years ago when Papa was in Japan. But why did we have to burn pictures of my grandparents just because they lived in Japan? "*Shikata ga nai*," Mama said, which means it cannot be helped. Mama says that about a lot of things.

I didn't want to go to school that Monday but Mama wouldn't budge. I didn't even eat breakfast, just drank my Ovaltine and ran for the bus with Naomi. On the bus I could feel everyone staring at us. I wanted to ask them why they didn't mind their own business, but Mama had made us promise to keep our eyes straight and our lips sealed. "Just act like you did before all this happened" were Mama's words of wisdom.

Naomi immediately took out her sketching pad and drew. I looked out the window. All the newsboys were hawking papers with WAR written across the whole top half in great big black letters. EXTRA, EXTRA, JAPS BOMB PEARL HARBOR, JAPS BOMB PEARL HARBOR, they shouted.

While I was getting off the bus, this fat old lady who had been looking at me the whole way asked if I was Chinese or Japanese. I said I was American and she spit at me and said, "Go back to Japan, where you belong." That's a laugh. Where I belong. I don't even know where Japan is.

I was so busy talking to that stupid lady that I left my slide rule, the one with the nice leather carrying case that Papa gave me for my birthday, on the seat.

Robbie was waiting outside. He could see I was upset. It's hard to fool Robbie about things like that. I told him what happened on the bus and he said I shouldn't let stuff like that bother me. "You didn't do anything wrong, Ben," he said. Up till then I didn't think I *had* done anything wrong.

Robbie insisted on walking with me to homeroom. He acts like he's my older brother sometimes. But he's smaller than me and, besides, I can take care of myself. He kept looking around like someone was going to attack us. I told him to take it easy. "Always expect the unexpected," he said. That's one of his favorite mottos.

He had a point though. Everyone in the entire school *was* staring at me, especially the big kids. Robbie said that everyone was talking about the eggs that someone threw at Mr. Tsukamoto's house and the headstones on the Japanese graves that got smashed last night. *Great,* I thought. *Only six more hours of school — if I live.*

Mr. Vale, my homeroom teacher, was watching me during the Pledge of Allegiance. Maybe he wanted to keep an eye on me in case I said "I pledge allegiance to Japan . . ." or something. I said it just the same as I usually do except I did mumble a little when I came to the "one nation indivisible . . ." part. That seemed particularly dumb. It didn't seem like one undivided nation that Monday. At least not in San Francisco.

I never thought I looked different from the other kids. Never once, even though most of them are Caucasian, except for Billy Smith, who's a Negro, and Charles Hamada, who's part Japanese, part jerk. But now I realized my face *was* different. My hair was black. My skin was yellow. My eyes were narrow. It never seemed to matter before, but it sure did matter now. Now my face was the face of the enemy.

When I got home, Mama and Papa were still sitting around the kitchen table listening to the radio. It was like they hadn't moved. I think they were hoping that there had been some kind of horrible mistake and that the announcer would break in with a bulletin and clear everything up so we could go back to our regular lives. But the news was only getting worse: Thousands of Americans had been killed and thousands more wounded.

I just went up to my room to read my Superman comic book until dinner was ready. I heard a car pull up and two men I never saw before got out. They were wearing hats pulled way down over their faces and raincoats, but it wasn't even raining.

When Papa opened the front door, the two men talked to him for a minute or two. They were talking real low so I couldn't hear what they were saying. Then they showed Papa their wallets — probably badges or something — and Papa let them in.

Papa didn't seem surprised by the visit. It was almost like he was expecting them. Same with Mama, but you could see she was more upset than Papa. Mama thinks she's good at hiding what she's thinking, but she isn't.

Naomi was right behind me, which I didn't realize until Mama waved us into the kitchen. Mama said that the men were going to take Papa away for a while so they could ask him some questions. That's just what she said, like she was telling us the weather for tomorrow. Cloudy with a chance of kidnapping.

Naomi didn't let Mama get away with that. She asked why they were taking Papa and where and for how long. Mama didn't want to answer any of Naomi's questions, but Naomi just stood there waiting for an answer. Mama said because of Pearl Harbor, the government was taking away any Japanese men it considered a danger to the country. Papa belonged to the Japanese Businessmen's Association that met on Thursday nights. The government is afraid that men like Papa might help the Japanese bomb California.

This didn't make sense to me. Why would anyone consider Papa dangerous? He was just an optometrist, which isn't a very dangerous occupation, if you ask me. And heaven help the Japanese if they needed Papa. What would he do, give all the pilots an eye exam? Besides, last year was his fiftieth birthday. He's too old. Just trying to picture Papa being a danger to the country makes me laugh. Well, it would if things weren't so unfunny.

I think it was a mistake saying all this to Mama, though. She sent us up to our rooms. We stopped at the top of the stairs so we could listen to what was going on. One of the men stayed in the living room with Papa. The other one was looking through all the rooms, even mine and Naomi's. He gave me a pat on the head and looked like he wanted to say something. But he didn't.

He took the sheets off the mattresses and turned them upside down; opened all the dresser drawers and threw everything on the floor; looked in all the closets and took out all the papers in Papa's desk and put them in big brown cardboard cartons along with his radio, camera, binoculars, and telescope. They hauled the cartons outside and put them in the trunk of the car, where a third man waited behind the wheel, smoking a cigarette.

They turned the whole house upside down looking for who knows what. It's a good thing Papa decided to burn all the Japanese stuff. There's no telling what would have happened if they found any of *that*.

After the men finished loading up the car, Papa came to talk to me and Naomi. Naomi wanted to know why Papa hadn't run away somewhere so the men couldn't find him. She was mad that Papa was just going to leave quietly with them. But Papa said there was no place to hide and that if he ran away he would worry about what the men would do to us.

Naomi always says the first thing that comes into her head. She's not a very thoughtful person, although she means well.

"The family must stick together so we can remain strong," Papa said, "like the chopsticks." He asked us if we remembered the chopsticks. Of course we did, because he told us about thirty thousand times. "It's easy to break one chopstick, but many chopsticks banding together will bend but not break." It's one of Robbie's favorites. He calls them Papa's Shogun Slogans. He and Papa really get along. Sometimes I think Papa likes Robbie more than he likes me.

We didn't cry when Papa left because we knew that would just make it harder for him and Mama.

The next Sunday I went to Robbie's to play football, the same as usual. Danny McManus, who's a jerk anyway, knocked me down with an elbow on the first play of the game. He did it on purpose. I know, because as I was getting up, he said, "That's what a Jap deserves."

Robbie asked me if I was all right. I didn't want Danny to know that he hurt me, even though my whole face was throbbing. I didn't say anything — just got up and went back to the huddle.

On the very next play, I called an end around to Danny's side. I took the handoff from Tommy, who hid the play perfectly. I had a clear shot all the way down to the parking lot, but I slowed down, looking for Danny.

Danny knew what I was doing, but there wasn't anything he could do about it. I'm too big and too fast. He was rooted to the spot and I hit him full force. You could hear the sound of bone on bone and the loud hiss as the air left his body. His head shot back, his legs shot forward, and he hit the ground with a terrible jolt.

For a minute I was afraid he might be dead, but he moved after a couple of seconds and got up, holding his mouth. His shirt was already soaked with blood. He looked at me like he wanted to say something. I just threw the ball at his bloodied face and said, "Second down, clown," and walked away.

Mama was upset when I got home because thanks to Danny's elbow, my eye was so swollen that it was half closed. She was sure something had happened, but I told her it was nothing, just an accident.

I figured she had enough to worry about.

After they took Papa away, we kept the shades down — even during the day — so the neighbors couldn't spy on us. You didn't know who to trust anymore. We spoke in whispers, and locked all the doors and windows at night, which we'd never done before.

Japanese warships were planning to attack the coast; planes had been spotted over Los Angeles. That's what people were saying, anyway.

You never knew what to expect. A boy my age was arrested because they thought his metal lunch box was a radio transmitter. The police were stopping Japanese people driving cars and asking them where they were going and what they were doing.

Chinese people were wearing buttons saying I'M CHINESE so that no one would think they were Japanese, and Japanese people were wearing the same buttons hoping no one would be the wiser. Naomi heard that Mr. Hirabayashi was going to a doctor to have his eyelids fixed so he wouldn't look Japanese.

One of the restaurants we used to go to has a sign in the window now that says: WE POISON BOTH JAPS AND RATS and the barber shop next door posted a sign announcing: WE SHAVE JAPS — NOT RESPONSIBLE FOR ACCIDENTS.

Cars go by with bumper stickers saying JAP HUNTING LICENSE: OPEN SEASON or JAPS DON'T LET THE SUN SHINE ON YOU: KEEP MOVING.

Our neighbor, Mrs. Watanabe, told Mama that Papa and the other men are being held as insurance in case the Japanese torture American prisoners of war. She said that some of the men were beaten by the FBI because they wouldn't confess to being spies and refused to rat on others. There was even talk that one man had been found dead, his body covered with bruises.

Each week the news got worse as the Japanese victories continued and the American losses mounted. Then, last week, we went from the frying pan into the fire — as Motto Man put it. I was coming home from school and I saw soldiers taping notices in store windows and nailing them to telephone poles. One of the words was so big I could see it from the bus: JAP.

I asked Mama if she knew what the notices said. She was silent for a moment. And then she spoke. She said that San Francisco had been declared a war zone and we were going to be evacuated. She didn't say where we were going or how long we were going to be there, just that we were going to be evacuated. Then she just looked at me like she was expecting me to say, "Oh, well, I'll just run up to my room and finish my homework so I won't be late for the evacuation."

I had a million questions but Mama looked like she was hoping I wouldn't ask any of them, so I just grabbed some leftover chicken and went upstairs.

I must have fallen asleep, because the next thing I knew it was 11:30 and Mama and Naomi were arguing in the kitchen. Mama was speaking a lot of Japanese, which drives Naomi crazy. I couldn't make out what they were saying, so I went downstairs and stood outside of the kitchen.

"We're going to be taken and put in a prison camp just because you and Papa were born in Japan. As if that's a crime. This 'innocent until proven guilty' junk doesn't apply if your parents are Japanese." Naomi was almost shouting — I had never heard her speak to Mama like this.

Before I realized what was happening, she stormed out of the kitchen and passed right by me. I was hoping she hadn't seen me, but halfway up the stairs she turned and said, "Do what you want, but I'm not going to school anymore."

The next day Mama came back from the Civil Control Station with a batch of tags all numbered 13559. We have to attach them to our luggage and hang one from our coat buttons when we leave. The man told Mama we can only take one duffel bag and two suitcases each. Mama was worried that we would be split up but he said that families would be allowed to stay together.

Before Mama went to the Civil Control Station, she took the sign Naomi painted and put it in the window of Papa's store.

Goodbye to all my customers. I will miss each of you and hope to return soon to serve you once again.

Very truly yours,
Masao Uchida

Me and Naomi said we would go with her, but Mama said she wanted to go alone.

Naomi said she doesn't get it either. Tommy La Motta's parents were born in Italy and they don't even speak English, but no one is making them pack up and move to a prison camp. I told her what Mrs. Watanabe said to Mama.

Mrs. Watanabe thinks the whole thing is a "disgrace." "Why are we being rounded up like we're criminals while the Germans and Italians come and go like nothing is happening?" she asks, and before Mama has a chance to open her mouth she answers, "Because we look different. The Germans and Italians are Caucasians and we are Orientals."

All Mama can say is "*shikatagani*," trying to convince Mrs. Watanabe to make the best of the situation. Mama's very Japanesey when it comes to things like this. But Naomi thinks she is just saying that because that's what Papa said we should do in his letter.

Now that Mama knows Papa is in Missoula, Montana, she isn't worried that we'll get separated from him forever. Many of the sentences in the letter we received from him were crossed out. It's kind of hard to understand that way.

Thursday Mama came back from downtown with even more bad news. The bank won't give her any of Papa's money. She pleaded with the man, but he just sat there shaking his head and saying there was nothing he could do because all Japanese bank accounts have been frozen by the government. He said we could have our money after the war.

We're selling everything. We need every cent, and anyway, there's no telling when we'll be back.

The man at the Civil Control Station told Mama that she could store any property she wanted with them and then reclaim it after the war. I'm *sure* they'll keep an eagle eye on our stuff while we're away. The government won't even let us have our own money, so why in the world would we trust them to keep our stuff safe? They say we have to leave so they can protect us from the people who hate us because of Pearl Harbor. I think most of the people who hate us are *in* the government.

The government sent a man to our house to take our furniture. He and the other men loaded everything onto a big truck and drove off with it. Now we have no place to sleep or eat. But we leave in two days, so I guess it doesn't matter.

Mama got only a few dollars from the man, but we had no choice. People are trying to take advantage of us. She even sold Papa's car for $20.

Mrs. Watanabe was so insulted by how little they offered that she took every glass and dish in the house and threw them against the living room wall until the floor was covered with broken bits and pieces. She even smashed all the fine dishes she got when she was married. She told Mama she would rather destroy everything she owned than let those "vultures" have it.

The government man went running out of Mrs. Watanabe's house yelling that she was a crazy woman. Mrs. Watanabe yelled right back, asking him who was crazier: her for smashing everything or him for thinking she would sell it all for $11?

Mama and Mrs. Watanabe talked about the night they took Papa away. Mr. Watanabe thinks the reason they took Papa and not him is because Papa belonged to the Japanese Businessmen's Association. Mr. Watanabe would never belong to anything like that — he's not Japanesey and old-fashioned, like Papa.

Mr. and Mrs. Watanabe look like brother and sister. They're even the same height. They not only look the same, they also act the same. They're not like Mama and Papa — they say what's on their minds.

Mama said Mrs. Watanabe's more upset than usual because she's going to have her first baby and doesn't want to have it wherever we're going. I don't blame her. I'm not even having a baby and I don't want to go wherever it is we're going.

Mr. Mills is the only one who has offered to help. He's

our landlord. Papa always said that Mr. Mills was a "fine man," and he turned out to be right. Mr. Mills told Mama not to worry about the rent and said that we could store things in his basement until we return.

We're nearly packed: sheets, towels, forks, knives, and spoons. We don't know what kind of clothes to take because we still have no idea where we're going or if the place is hot or cold.

Naomi heard that they're going to load us in a big ship, sail it out to the middle of the ocean, and blow it up.

Swell country, if you ask me.

Mrs. Watanabe's mother has to remain behind. She is in the hospital because of her heart. The doctor said it was too dangerous for her to travel. Mrs. Watanabe wanted to take her so that she could care for her properly.

Mrs. Yamashiro's son can't go either. He's retarded and has been taken somewhere — a hospital or something. Mrs. Yamashiro has always taken care of him at home. But the man said she will not be able to take care of him where she is going.

Mrs. Murase *is* going, even though she doesn't have to. She is Caucasian and Mr. Murase is Japanese. She doesn't have to go but what would she do, stay here and let her husband and three children go alone?

The only one who's happy about all this is Charles Hamada. This is going to be "loads of fun," according to him. He said it'll be like camping in the woods. I asked him if he had ever camped in the woods and, of course, he hasn't. He's not exactly playing with a full deck if you ask me.

The only thing he's concerned about is Cheeseball. That's his stupid cat. He's really worked himself into a lather about it. We're not allowed to take pets with us — probably because it's not safe for pets, which are apparently rated higher than Japanese humans by the American government.

Charles only has two more days to find a home for Cheeseball. He doesn't have a prospect in sight even though he put an ad in the paper last week.

Last night a man called and told Naomi he was going to set fire to the house if we didn't get out soon. If that wasn't enough, Mr. Korematsu was found hanging from the ceiling of his flower store yesterday.

Naomi talked to his daughter, who's in her class. She said that at first her father thought all this evacuation stuff was some kind of joke. He went around asking if it was true and no matter how many times everyone assured him that it was, he didn't believe them. He laughed and told them they were mistaken. "This is America," he would say.

He locked the store, put chains on the front door, and nailed wooden beams across the windows. He must have been there for days, because when they finally broke in, all the flowers were dead, too.

Tomorrow we leave.

Thursday, April 23, 1942
On a train

I'm writing this on the floor, in between cars. No one knows I'm here, otherwise I would get in trouble. Mama and Naomi and everyone else are still sleeping. The train didn't leave for a long time because there were so many people who had to get on board. The only thing I know is it's near dawn now. I came back here to get some light so I could write.

When we got downtown to the assembly area, there were thousands of Japanese people around, all wearing numbered identification tags just like we were. There must have been a million suitcases and duffel bags piled up all along the sidewalk — some of the kids were playing hide-and-seek around them. One little girl held her mama's coat in one hand and an American flag in the other.

Almost everyone was wearing their Sunday best — like they were going to church or a fancy party. Some of the ladies held handkerchiefs up to their faces so they could hide their tears.

I was glad Mama wasn't crying like they were. She was too busy looking around, her eyes slowly scanning from side to side, afraid she might miss something. Usually Mama's eyes are downcast, in that Japanesey way she has. But not then. She knew that without Papa, we had only her to depend on.

They were serving coffee and sugared doughnuts by the building next to the train tracks. But just as we got to the table with the doughnuts, the crowd started to surge toward the train, which was huffing and crackling like it was getting ready to go.

Some of the old people had to be helped on to the train because the stairs were too high. One family had so many little ones they had to be handed up one at a time. The papa had a bag of baby stuff strapped to his back. He held the infant while he handed one of the kids up to the mama and then hurried back to get one of the other two before they got trampled or crawled away. The last one was hugging a big brown bear. He wasn't about to give it up to anyone in or out of the government.

We had to walk quite a ways before we found a car with room. Me and Naomi got on first and helped Mama up. Mama was worried about our bags, but I showed her the soldiers loading everything onto one of the cars at the back. We sat in the first empty seats we came to. The train was old and smelled bad.

The man in front of us was upset about something and was talking very fast to the lady who was sitting with him. They had a boy who was crying that he wanted Night-Night. He called the lady *obasan*, aunt. She wasn't his mama. I couldn't figure out what they were saying because the man was talking too fast in Japanese. I can understand some Japanese — a word here or there and maybe a sentence or two, but not the way he was talking.

I asked Mama what the man was so upset about. Mama leaned over and whispered so close in my ear that her breath tickled me. She said that the man's wife had gone to Japan and taken his only daughter with her. They wanted her to meet her grandparents and they were on a ship coming back to America when the Japanese bombed Pearl Harbor and they had to turn back. That was the last he had heard from them and he doesn't know where they are and is worried that she will not know where he and his little boy are. I told Mama I thought that was a sad story and she said it was.

All night I listened to the creak and clatter of the train. Sometimes the lights went out and I sat there, staring into the blackness. The air in the car was stuffy and stale. I could smell people being sick.

In the middle of the night someone threw a brick through one of the windows. The loud noise sounded like an explosion and woke everyone. All the little kids started crying, but no one was hurt. The brick landed in the aisle.

The train is slowing down now. It's getting lighter. There are loud footsteps above me and soldiers are running up and down outside, along the tracks, shouting.

We're here.

Friday, April 24, 1942
Mirror Lake, California

So many things are happening I thought I'd better write some of them down before I forget.

When I got off the train, the first thing I thought was they must have let us off at the wrong stop. This wasn't even a *stop*. There was just flatness as far as the eye could see. There was nothing growing anywhere — not a tree, a bush, or a flower. Nothing.

Then I realized there was something. I thought it must be a mirage, but it wasn't. It was a town — not a regular town, but about a thousand neat rows of identical army barracks that seemed to go on forever.

They were enclosed by a really high fence that had barbed wire on the top. The barbed wire sloped inward so you knew it was to stop people from getting out, not from getting in. There were signs saying: ELECTRIFIED FENCE: STAND BACK. They were in English. Since a lot of the old folks didn't read English, I thought that was particularly considerate of the people who put them up.

And if that didn't convince us not to make a run for it, there were watchtowers with soldiers pointing machine guns down at us. In between the two tallest watchtowers, there were these huge entrance gates with a red, white, and blue sign over them:

I'll bet the person who made that sign thought he was really clever, writing Mirror Lake that way. I wonder where the lake is.

People started drifting toward the gates and forming a line. The line moved real slow. We were all going into a building with another big sign on it. ADMINISTRATION, the sign said.

Once I got into the administration building, I was frisked by a soldier. I told him I left my tank at home, but he didn't think that was funny. Most soldiers don't have a sense of humor. If you did you could never be a soldier — not a good one, anyway.

Mama filled out a medical examination form, which me and Naomi helped her with. Then I went into a half booth where I had to undress. When I came out, a nurse told me to stick my tongue out and say *aaahhh*, so she could jam a stick halfway down my throat. She didn't even look at me when she said, "You're fine. Next."

One of the soldiers said we should go identify our luggage. I was really hungry and hoping we could eat. All we had on the train was a box of crackers Mama brought and some oranges they handed out. But it looked like we would have to wait.

We left Mama in the shade and went off to find our stuff, which turned out to be somewhere in this mile-high pile of duffel bags, boxes, and suitcases. Miraculously I spotted the duffel bag Mr. Mills lent us. That was the good news. The bad news was that now I had to figure out some way to get it down.

I decided to pretend I was BEN UCHIDA: WORLD-FAMOUS MOUNTAIN CLIMBER ATTEMPTING, FOR THE FIRST TIME IN RECORDED HISTORY, TO

CLIMB — UNASSISTED, UNACCOMPANIED, AND
WITHOUT A NET — MOUNT LUGGAGE.

After a few minor spills I made it down with our bags.
Then another soldier went through them looking for anything that wasn't supposed to be there: knives, flashlights,
cameras, bombs — stuff like that. I thought about telling
him my tank joke, but he didn't look any funnier than the
other guy.

He asked me if we knew our "housing assignment" and
I said we didn't. He said I should go find out and come
back and tell him, so he could make sure our luggage got
taken there. He was pretty nice, actually.

While we were away, Mama *had* found out our "housing
assignment." We were in Block B, Barrack 14, Apartment E.

Each row of barracks and the dirt roads in between
looked *exactly* the same to me. There were no signs anywhere. It looked like they had just finished building the
place about ten minutes before we arrived. We kept
walking around in circles until some people helped us
find Block B.

Apartment E was just an empty room, that's all. The
only things in it were these cots with empty sacks and
blankets folded on top and a big iron coal stove in the
middle of the floor. A lone lightbulb dangled from the

ceiling. There were no tables, no chairs, no kitchen, and no bathroom.

If Mama hadn't spoken first we all might still be standing there. "Get a bucket and a broom," she said.

Sure, I thought, I'll just run down to the corner hardware store and bring back a bucket and broom. Where did Mama think I was going to get anything like that out here in the middle of nowhere? But I could tell from the look on Mama's face that it was best I figured out the answer to that real soon.

We decided that the administration building was a good place to start.

Naomi went up to a kid her age and asked him where she could get a bucket and a broom. That's one of the things I like about Naomi. She's not afraid of anything, except snakes. I think the guy thought Naomi was pretty cute, which she is in a weird sort of way. He said he would "be back in a flash" and winked. Naomi didn't pay much attention to any of it. That's the way she is.

When he came out, he actually had a bucket and a broom. I had to give the guy credit. He said that his name was Mike Masuda and then winked at Naomi again. Naomi's always real polite, so she said, "I'm Naomi, and this is my little brother, Ben." I could have killed her when she said that.

Mike's dad works in the administration building. He said we should let him know anytime we need something. Sounds like the kind of guy who can come in handy in a place like this.

You would have thought we brought Mama a dozen red roses the way she brightened up when she saw the bucket and broom. I found a piece of cardboard outside, which we used to get all the dust we swept up into the bucket. There was so much dust that the bucket was almost filled to the top when I took it outside to dump it. I took it pretty far away, but even as I was dumping it the wind was blowing it all back.

When I returned, Naomi said we had to find where the straw was so we could fill our sacks or else we wouldn't have anything to sleep on tonight. Mama said we should bring back some water, too, since there wasn't even a sink in our "apartment."

Not far away was a straw pile with hundreds of Japanese around it frantically filling their sacks. By the time I was finished, the sweat was streaming down my face. The wind was blowing hard and the dust was flying all over the place. I tried to keep my eyes shut as much as I could, but the dust got in anyway.

We found a spigot right near the laundry area, washed out the bucket real good, and filled it with water. When we got back, the man and the boy — the ones who were sitting in front of us on the train — were standing outside our apartment. The man nodded to me and I winked at the boy. He wasn't crying just then but he looked like it wouldn't take much.

Inside, Mama and the aunt were talking. The aunt was explaining to Mama that they too had been assigned to Block B, Barrack 14, Apartment E. You could tell that this wasn't the first time the aunt had tried to explain this to Mama. Mama was saying that she must have made a mistake. Mama said that it wasn't possible for all six of us to share this small apartment and that the aunt should go back to the administration building and get the *right* housing site. But the aunt stood her ground just as firmly as Mama did. She explained to Mama that this was the way it was all over. That all the apartments were being shared by more than one family.

Frankly, I figured, it could have been worse. We could have been bunking with Charles Hamada and his family. If that happened, I would just head for the old electrified fence and end it right then and there.

The boy's father came in and said he had an idea. He could see that his sister and Mama were upset and if the situation didn't get better real quick, it was going to get a whole lot worse. He left and when he came back he had some rope which he strung across the middle of the room. Then he hung the blankets that were piled on the cots over it so that the apartment was now divided in two. "We can have a little privacy, now," the man said to Mama, kindly, in Japanese. Mama thanked him but could say no more.

Monday, May 4, 1942

I don't think I slept more than five minutes in a row the whole week. Every morning when I get up I wonder if I went to sleep at all. Last night I was up all night thinking about my room back home. I never realized how quiet our street was. Sometimes a car would drive by or a couple coming from the movie theater would be talking real loud, but that was pretty much it.

Here if it's not one thing, it's another. Jimmy, Mr. Tashima's boy, has been crying pretty much nonstop. He keeps saying that he misses his mama and wants to go back home and see "Night-Night," whoever that is. Aunt Mitsuko does her best to comfort him, but she makes almost as much noise trying to quiet him as he does. I almost prefer the crying.

Last night Jimmy was quiet, much to my amazement. I thought I might actually get some sleep. But just as I was dozing off, an argument started up in the apartment next to ours. The walls are so thin you can hear every sound. There's nothing you can do about it.

Of course, sleeping on these cots is enough to keep anyone awake. Right now, I'm on the floor. It's the only place I can write. I have to stop now because if you don't get in line early for breakfast you're just out of luck.

Wednesday, May 6, 1942

I got lost again today. I feel like a mouse in a maze. Maybe that's really what this is — some kind of bizarre secret experiment run by the government. They want to see how long it will take the average twelve-year-old kid to go crazy because he has to spend all day running around in circles just to find his way back to where he lives.

Every building looks the same as *every* other building and *every* street looks the same as *every* other street. You'd think they could at least put up some signs. Even in prison they tell you what cell block you're in.

Thursday, May 7, 1942

Every day after breakfast me and Naomi go down and watch the next train come in. We were the first ones to arrive, but more are coming each day. Three hundred today. Five hundred tomorrow. We ran into Mike and he came with us. I think he wants to see Naomi more than the train.

It sure is strange seeing all these Japanese faces. Except

for the soldiers and a few government types lurking around, everyone except for Mrs. Murase is Japanese. You would think we'd taken the train all the way to Tokyo.

We're not the only ones who watch the trains come in. Lots of people do. They're looking for anyone they know: family, friends. Everyone, it seems, is from somewhere in California.

The people who got off the train today looked about as tired and confused as we did that first day. Some were so sick they had to be lifted through the windows on stretchers. There was even a blind guy on yesterday's train. And another guy wearing his World War I U.S. Army uniform. A lot of good that's going to do him.

The place is really filling up. Soon they'll have to put up a NO VACANCY sign. The lines at the mess hall are much longer than when we first got here, that's for sure. The wait is so bad they've set up tents because some of the ladies who are even older than Mama are fainting from the heat of the noonday sun. There isn't much shade here in Mirror Lake.

Friday, May 8, 1942

Naomi says she heard Mr. Tashima talking with Mr. Watanabe. Mr. Watanabe said we are about three hundred miles or so northeast of San Francisco, but no one really knows. No one even knows where the nearest town is.

Saturday, May 9, 1942

Tomorrow is Mother's Day. I don't know if Mama just wants to forget it or not. Papa always brought home a bunch of chrysanthemums from Mr. Korematsu's flower shop, so I know it's going to be a sad day. Even if we could get some for her, it wouldn't be the same. Naomi is making a card with a drawing of chrysanthemums on the front.

She thinks we should both sign it and give it to Mama in the morning.

Monday, May 11, 1942

Jimmy kept everyone up again crying for Night-Night. Naomi asked Aunt Mitsuko who Night-Night was. She said he was their Labrador puppy. Jimmy named him that because at bedtime he would say "night-night" and the puppy would circle round, curl up into a little ball, and sleep next to his bed until morning, when he licked Jimmy awake.

They had to leave Night-Night with the people who lived upstairs. Aunt Mitsuko said Jimmy's been crying ever since.

Thursday, May 14, 1942

We need more blankets and I mean soon. Maybe Mike can get us some. I had to take all my clothes out of the suitcase and cover myself with them last night. It's hot during the day because the black tar paper that covers the outside soaks up the sun. But at night it's cold. No wonder no one lives here on purpose.

Mr. Tashima, Jimmy's father, said he would have the coal stove working by tomorrow night. I sure hope so. Mr. Tashima is a carpenter. We're really lucky. He's making a table and chairs so we can all have something to sit on. I'm going to help him get lumber from the scrap heap and nails that we can straighten out and use again. He showed me where there's a big pile of lumber that must have been left over by whoever built Mirror Lake. Mr. Tashima said I should take whatever I can carry. After he finishes the table and chairs he's going to make a chest of drawers, so we can all stop living out of suitcases and getting our stuff from under the cots.

Monday, May 18, 1942

Mess hall is definitely the right word for where we eat. Officially it's the Dining Hall. That's a laugh. We're just one step away from feed bags and they want to call it the Dining Hall. As if the chandeliers are going to be installed any day now.

We have to bring our knives, forks, and spoons with us, otherwise we have to eat with our fingers, which would be all right with me. Each morning Mama wipes our forks and spoons clean from the dust with the skirt of her dress. Jimmy's been watching Mama do this and this morning he came up to her holding his fork and spoon saying, "clean, clean." When she finished he broke out in a giant smile — the first one I've seen. He's a good kid, especially since his mama's not here and he can't have any idea what's going on.

This morning each line leading into the mess hall was

as long as a San Francisco city block. If they get any longer it'll be lunch by the time we get to breakfast.

Now that the place is full, you spend all day in line. We waited in one line for half an hour yesterday only to find out it didn't lead anywhere. So we had to go to the rear of another line and wait another half an hour.

And that's just the beginning. After you're inside you have to wait in line until they dump the food into your stupid tin plate. The plate's divided into three parts: one big part and two little ones for your vegetables and dessert, I guess. We had liver with a scoop of canned string beans today. Yum.

The mess hall is even bigger than the school cafeteria back home, but not nearly as nice. And boy, is it noisy. Everyone wanders around with their trays, looking for a place to sit, while about eight million kids run up and down the aisles, yelling and ignoring their mamas, who try to make them behave.

When I was taking my plate up to the dishwashing counter, I saw Mike. He recognized me right away and asked me where my "big sister" was. She was still eating and I pointed with my tray, which was a big mistake because everything almost fell off. I asked him about the blankets and he said he would see what he could do.

Wednesday, May 20, 1942

Aunt Mitsuko speaks English with an even worse Japanese accent than Mama. Sometimes I can't understand a word she's saying. At least she and Mama *try*. A lot of the old folks here don't speak any English. Not a word.

Friday, May 22, 1942

Mr. Tashima said we should be careful with the stove because the sparks could set the barracks on fire and it would spread quickly. It would take about four minutes for this place to go up in smoke. Four minutes and it's bye-bye, Mirror Lake. "Food for thought," as Robbie would say.

Monday, May 25, 1942

Mr. Tashima built a hobbyhorse for Jimmy that he made from some logs. Jimmy's decided he wants me to show him how to ride. Each night before bedtime we play a little bucking bronco. I think it helps him get to sleep. At least he's stopped crying for Night-Night.

Mr. Tashima also carved nameplates that he nailed up outside our apartment. One says UCHIDA and the other,

TASHIMA. He found a saw blade one of the workers must have left behind and used that. He's a real magician when it comes to wood. I suggested he might consider building us a plane so we could all fly out of here. That got a good laugh out of him. I like to see Mr. Tashima laugh every once in a while. He is very serious most of the time.

Naomi said that she heard Aunt Mitsuko telling Mama that he isn't always like this. It's just that he's worried about his wife and daughter.

Monday, June 1, 1942

I got separated from everyone at breakfast and was looking around for a place to sit — which can be a real pain — when, from way over on the other side of the mess hall, I heard someone saying, "Uchida! Uchida!" I knew in an instant it had to be Charles Hamada. I knew it was Charles because he always calls people by their last names.

He was waving like a madman and flashing that idiotic smile he has. I pretended not to hear him, hoping he would go away. But Charles wasn't going to go away, no matter what. The longer I ignored him, the louder he called my name. People were starting to turn around to see who he was calling.

There really wasn't much room at Charles's table but I managed to squeeze in, no thanks to the rest of the

Hamadas. There were scars all over Charles's face. It seems that when Charles finally found someone to take Cheeseball, Cheeseball decided that he had no intention of going anywhere peacefully. When Charles attempted to hand him over, the cat grabbed a chunk of his cheek and held on for dear life. Charles said they had quite a time convincing him to let go, and from the look of Charles's face, he ain't lyin'.

When Charles was done eating, he started putting his knife, fork, and spoon back into this little burlap bag. I couldn't help it, I had to find out what he was doing. He said his mama gave him the bag so his "utensils" didn't get all dusty on the way to the mess hall.

That was it. I couldn't stand it anymore, and I told Charles I was going up for seconds. Charles looked at me like I was crazy — and he did have a point. Not only would I have to elbow my way through all the people still wearily wandering the aisles looking for a friendly face and an empty seat, but who in his right mind would want second helpings of canned sausages? Boy, I'd give my right arm for a hamburger, fries, a Coke, and a Baby Ruth.

I told Charles I was sure I'd see him around, hoping to make a clean getaway, but no such luck. He asked me what block I was in so he could come visit. I didn't have a choice. I lied.

Wednesday, June 3, 1942

Last night I was eating dinner — if you want to call it that — and Mike tapped me on the shoulder and asked if he could sit next to me. I thanked him for the blankets and slid over because I figured he just wanted to talk to Naomi. But it turns out he wanted to talk to me. He said he heard I was a real good center fielder, which I was, but how did he know?

I said, "Yeah, so?" and he said they were starting a baseball league and he was in Block B, too, so we were going to be on the same team.

I had to admit this was the best thing I had heard since I made the mistake of getting off that train. I hadn't heard anything about any baseball league. He said there was going to be a team meeting and practice after breakfast tomorrow and he hoped I would be there. I couldn't believe that this guy knew I could play center field. Naturally I said sure, I'd be there, and I asked him what position he wanted to play. He said he was going to pitch. Not that he *wanted* to pitch, but that he was *going* to pitch. The guy doesn't exactly lack confidence.

When I got back to the apartment, I turned the place upside down looking for my mitt and cap. They were the first things I packed but I couldn't remember *un*packing them. Then I remembered the duffel bag, which was under the bed. I found my mitt, but no cap.

I was pretty unhappy about the cap. It was my favorite, not just because of the Dodgers or even because I always told everyone the B was for Ben, not Brooklyn, but because Robbie had *the same exact one*. I just couldn't remember if I took it or not. I had a few other things on my mind at the time.

To be on the safe side, I slept on the mitt.

friday, June 12, 1942

Mike can really pitch. I don't mean throw, I mean *pitch*. He's got good speed, and I've never seen anyone with so much control. He can put the ball anywhere he wants. We played a practice game today and I got a single off him, but he had me leaning most of the time. He's better than any of the guys back home, and we had some good guys on the team.

Kenny Okada is a great first baseman and a good leadoff hitter. Ricky Yatabe bats second and plays left. Of course I bat third and play center field.

I thought maybe I had lost it a little, but as soon as I got out there and chased down some flies I felt better. I'm still fast enough that I can play really shallow. Mike says he's watched some of the other teams and we've got a good chance to go all the way to the championship.

Monday, June 15, 1942

Mama and Aunt Mitsuko are getting along better now. It makes things a lot easier. At first, I think, they were both ashamed because we all had to live crammed together in this lousy apartment, and they had no one to blame but each other. But now they laugh and talk Japanese just like they were sisters. I'm glad for Mama. Not having Papa is hard, especially for her. Every day when Aunt Mitsuko comes back from the post office, Mama's lids lower and she presses her lips real tight. I think she's trying not to cry. We all miss Papa. Naomi did a sketch of him and tacked it up on the wall. It helps because it's amazing how fast you forget what someone looks like. Even someone you've known your whole life. Like Papa.

Friday, June 9, 1942

Naomi's face was all chalky white when she woke up. She looked like a ghost. She said I wouldn't think it was so funny if I could see my own face in the mirror. The sand is *everywhere*. It still finds a way to come in during the night even though me and Mr. Tashima stuffed every slit, crack, and knothole in the place with paper. It must have taken about two days to build this place — that's what Mr. Tashima says.

During the day Mama, Naomi, and Aunt Mitsuko wear bandanas to keep the dust from getting in their hair. It doesn't work completely — nothing does. Sometimes, in the late afternoon, I can see a dust cloud forming in the far distance. When it reaches the barracks area you can't see ten feet in front of you.

Sunday, June 18, 1942

Mr. Tashima has finished our table and chairs. He's no ordinary carpenter, especially since he had to use a rock as a hammer because he couldn't find a real one. I'm sitting at the table now and it's really much nicer than the floor.

He's starting on a chest of drawers tomorrow. He's finally found some tools, so he thinks it will go much faster. He likes to have Jimmy with him when he works around here. All Jimmy needs is a block of wood and he's a happy guy.

We're lucky we're with the Tashimas. I've heard other people talk about the families they live with and I wouldn't want to trade places. One family yells at their kids under a blanket because they think then no one will overhear them.

Monday, June 21, 1942

Just my luck. I ran into Charles Hamada again today. I was with Mike. He was helping me get some scrap lumber for Mr. Tashima.

Charles said he was *so* glad he found me, like I was some kind of buried treasure. He had been looking all over for me. He had gone to Block C, Barrack 13, Apartment D just like I told him, and there was no one there who had *ever even heard of me*. He looked truly baffled.

I told Charles that he must have remembered wrong, because I live in Block *B*, Barrack *14*, Apartment *E*. I decided to just tell him the truth. This sent him into a major tailspin. Charles doesn't like to get things wrong. I once saw him answer a geometry question wrong back home and I thought he was going to jump out the window. He started to get the lonely look. I don't know how he manages to look so lonely but he really, really does. You just have to look away when he does that.

He asked me what I was doing and I told him. I never stopped walking the whole time, hoping he would get the hint, which of course he didn't. He asked if he could help and, since I didn't see any way out of it, I was about to say okay, when Mike said, "We don't need no help, pal." Mike's not real shy.

Charles looked like he wanted to say something but

changed his mind. He just hunched up his shoulders, sunk his head down in that pathetic way he has, and walked away. It kind of made me feel bad.

"He'll live," Mike said. "C'mon, the faster we get the wood for *ojisan* the faster we can play some ball." Mike thinks Mr. Tashima's my uncle and no matter how many times I tell him he isn't, he still calls him my uncle. I've pretty much given up.

Tuesday, June 20, 1942

I have to write to Robbie. He's probably mad by now. But I can't do both — keep up this journal and write long letters like he does. Besides, after I write this stuff I don't feel much like writing it all again. Most of it's pretty boring and the rest is worse than boring.

Thursday, June 22, 1942

One of the million things that's really strange about this place is that there are no pets. Not even a goldfish. I told Mike we should try and catch something so we can have a pet. He thought a snake might be nice. I'm sure Naomi would love it if we had a nice pet python. I'm not sure where pythons live, but I wouldn't be surprised if they were here in Mirror Lake.

Saturday, June 27, 1942

Mama and Aunt Mitsuko were talking about the toilets again last night. They're angry that there are no doors in the stalls. Mama said she is going to make curtains so she can hang them up every time she goes. Naomi told them that she just goes out into the field whenever she wants privacy. I don't know how I kept from laughing out loud when I heard that.

Monday, June 29, 1942

If me, Mike, and Kenny hadn't cut the line and snuck into dinner tonight, we would have died of starvation without a doubt. Sometimes the lines are so long it doesn't even pay to go eat. Mama is upset that I didn't eat with her, but it's just too boring sitting there with her, Naomi, and Aunt Mitsuko. Even Mr. Tashima doesn't eat with them all the time. Sometimes he sits with the other men, so I figure there's nothing wrong with us eating together, too.

We had a practice game against Block D. We won 12–0 and Mike didn't even pitch. We played on the field that's right near one of the guard towers. The guard looked happy to see us. I think most of them are pretty bored most of the time. In the fourth I came up with the bases loaded and he yelled out, "Hit a homer, kid," so, on the first pitch, I did. As I rounded the bases he took his helmet off to salute me and I waved to him after I touched home plate.

Naomi came by right after I hit the homer. She said she was disappointed that she didn't see it but I don't know about that. She didn't look so disappointed sitting on the bench talking a mile a minute to Mike. All the guys were looking at Mike, but he's not the type to care what other people think.

Our opening game is in just a couple of weeks. I can't wait.

Wednesday, July 1, 1942

Mr. Tashima has been appointed block manager. Only American citizens can be block managers, so that rules out all *Issei*. They were born in Japan, so they couldn't become American citizens even if they wanted to. But Mr. Tashima was born right here, in California, so he's already a citizen.

He gets paid sixteen dollars a month and has to keep track of the cleaning supplies; he also makes sure the area is picked up, repairs the barracks if needed, organizes the work groups, goes to all the meetings, and distributes official announcements and regulations. He doesn't mind doing the cleaning and repair, but he doesn't like all the other stuff.

Mr. Watanabe came by to talk to Mr. Tashima. He wanted him to know how glad he was that he was chosen. Mr. Watanabe said that there are lots of things the administration should be doing and Mr. Tashima was someone who truly understood the needs of the Japanese people and could speak on their behalf.

Mr. Tashima said he still didn't understand why the administration picked him, and Mr. Watanabe said it was because he spoke good English and got along with everyone. That made Mr. Tashima laugh. He said that was what he was worried about. That now that he was block manager, maybe he wouldn't get along with everyone so well.

Mr. Tashima is right to worry. Things have changed. It's not like it was during the first couple of months. Then everyone was just trying to figure out what was up and what was down. Some of the men are upset about not getting the good jobs. They complain that the good jobs were taken by the first to arrive and that they didn't have a fair chance.

People want the administration to make improvements: fix the sewers, make the latrines more private, improve the food, make the lines go quicker. Those are the kinds of things Mr. Watanabe is always talking about. There are more meetings now and more arguments.

Friday, July 3, 1942

Well, tomorrow's the big day. We're actually going to have a Fourth of July celebration right here in Barbed Wire City. Like Independence Day is something we should actually celebrate.

Sunday, July 5, 1942

Well, they did it. They had their Fourth of July celebration. The Boy Scout band was leading the parade — if you can call what they were doing "leading." They *were* marching, I will say that. Marching all over the place, blowing their bugles, banging their drums, and generally making fools of themselves.

There was a carnival, a full-fledged picnic with roasted wieners, relay races, a fashion show, and a beauty contest that wasn't half bad. I didn't know there were so many pretty girls here. They must have come from the other side of the camp, because it's the first time I've seen any of them.

Jimmy's nursery school class did a dance. They cut newspapers into long strips and colored them red, white, and blue — naturally. Then they made them into long paper chains which they were supposed to weave around themselves as they danced. Unfortunately a lot of the kids were bobbing when they should have been weaving, and some of them fell down because their little legs got all tangled up in the newspaper chain, and then the rest fell on top of them, laughing themselves silly. They looked like they were having a pretty good time, though.

But the highlight was the project director's speech. That's one of the things I love about this place. Nothing is called what it is. I mean this guy, Josselit, is the project director. Not the *prison camp* director or the warden. Of course, I'm living in a place called Mirror Lake where there's no lake, so what can you expect?

He told us this was a "glorious opportunity." That we had been "called upon" — I just loved that, "called upon," like God himself had come down from on high and asked us Japanese to do him a really big favor and spend the rest of our lives in the middle of nowhere — we had been "called upon" to come together here in Mirror Lake and show the world that we were not traitors but "as patriotic as anyone else in America."

The speech lasted about twenty-five lifetimes. Aunt Mitsuko had fallen asleep about three seconds after she sat down. Luckily, Mama's shoulder was holding her up, otherwise she would have been on the ground. Mama, of course, was staring straight ahead like this was the most interesting thing she had ever heard. But I know that look, and it means she isn't listening to a word.

It was an inspiring speech. I was inspired to think of different ways I could kill myself so I didn't have to listen to it. At one point Josselit got going so good he was starting to believe it himself. I thought he was going to get down on his knees and start wailing away, but he kind of ran out of steam. He looked like he was about to wrap things up when one of his assistants handed him a sheet of paper. He couldn't read it, partially because he's half blind — he had to take his glasses on and off every three seconds during the speech. I mean the guy is *old*. But not only that, a dust storm decided to kick up at that precise moment and had reached gale-force velocity by the time the assistant brought up the paper, which kept flapping around madly no matter how hard he tried to smack it down. If the assistant hadn't come back up and held the damn thing down, we would still be there.

Because someone had thrown a sparkler earlier that set the roof of Barrack 17 on fire, there wasn't going to be any fireworks show. That was the announcement. Mostly I went to the stupid Fourth of July thing just so I could see the fireworks. Besides, it wasn't such a big fire. They put it out in a minute.

Thursday, July 9, 1942

A letter from Robbie.

> *Ben —*
>
> *Are you there? Have you gotten this?*
>
> *It took me all this time to find out where they took you. They said you were at Mirror Lake. What on earth is Mirror Lake? I looked on every map of California I could find, and I don't see it.*
>
> *Are you having a good time or a bad time, check one. How's the swimming, by the way?*
>
> *Robbie*

Friday, July 10, 1942

Mr. Tashima said they're making desks and chairs as fast as they can. School starts Monday, even though nothing will be ready by then.

At first I thought Mr. Tashima was pulling my leg, but he didn't look like he was joking. You know, if there was one thing I liked about this place, it was that there was no school. Well, you can kiss that good-bye.

I asked him why we couldn't start school in September like we usually did back home. I thought that was a really good question. But Mr. Tashima said they had a parents' meeting last night and everyone was concerned because so much school time had been lost already. I asked him why we're going to school if we're going to spend the rest of our lives in Mirror Lake. I mean, what was the point? I thought that was an even better question than the first one. But Mr. Tashima just laughed and said he was sure we weren't going to be spending the rest of our lives in Mirror Lake.

I don't know what makes him think that; I've heard that we're *never* getting out of here. That the government didn't spend all this money to build Mirror Lake just so all the Japanese in California could get together and spend a couple of weeks camping out. Some say we're going to be used as hostages in case the Japanese capture American soldiers and make them prisoners of war — to make sure the Americans aren't mistreated. Then after that they're going to use us for target practice.

Tuesday, July 14, 1942

The siren goes off at seven and school starts at eight, so we have to get to the mess hall and out real quick. Fortunately, it isn't too far to school, if you know what I mean. And it isn't exactly what I would call a school. It's just the rec hall — or Wreck Hall, as I prefer to think of what they call the recreation barrack. They do have a sign up, though, I have to say that. It says MIRROR LAKE SCHOOL. As Motto Man would say, "Saying it's so don't make it so."

Even Jimmy has to go, which is making him unhappy because he doesn't like to leave Aunt Mitsuko. I think it's because he misses his mama. The only thing that helps is that he likes to follow me wherever I go, so I get to take him to school. I don't mind most of the time. I do it because it makes him smile, but I don't see why Naomi can't do it some of the time. Mama says that she's busy doing her drawing. Naomi doesn't even go to breakfast in the morning. She just wanders around the camp with her drawing pad and pencils.

Wednesday, July 15, 1942

I don't know which is worse: my classroom or my teacher. There's nothing to sit on and nothing to write on. Right now they bring in benches from the mess hall every morning. We use them as desks and sit on the floor.

There must be about sixty kids in my class. It's so crowded that some kids have to stand up and write their lessons up against the wall. There are no blackboards and no books. A school without books, what an interesting idea. Like a circus without elephants.

Miss Kroll — she's my teacher — just stands there all day and talks as loud as she can for as long as she can.

The noise is unbelievable. The only thing separating us from Mike's class, which is next door, is a thin piece of plywood that doesn't even go all the way up to the ceiling. The noise is so bad that this morning Miss Kroll had to stand on the top of her desk so we could hear her. The whole world is doing its best to blast each other to smithereens and we're supposed to be interested in the average rainfall in Guatemala. Who's kidding who?

Anyway, she was standing on the desk, asking what the capital of Illinois was, and someone in the next room, where the eighth-grade class sits, yelled out "Chicago," which cracked everyone up in both classes.

Saturday, July 18, 1942

A letter from Robbie.

> *Ben —*
>
> *Here's your cap. I bet you're wondering where I got it.*
>
> *Well, the last day of school, Mr. McCarthy summoned me up to the front of the room with that crooked finger move he thinks is so swell.*

"Your presence is requested in the principal's office," he said. *My guess was that they had found out that Chris V. gave me the answer to the science test essay question: What is the difference between the periodic table and a pool table? (Answer: A pool table is fun and a periodic table isn't.)*

As soon as I got to Mr. Maly's, they said I should go right in, which wasn't a good sign. Commander Maly was sitting behind his huge desk, and before I even had a chance to sit down he said, "Have you heard from your friend Uchida yet?"

I told him I'd gotten a letter from you. I decided to keep a low profile until he told me what he really wanted. It looked like it was going to take all day. He just sat there, peering over his idiotic half glasses and playing with a pile of junk on his desk.

Then it came to me. Junk? On Mr. Maly's desk? Robbie, I said to myself, There is something wrong with this picture. *Maly was sitting in his high-backed swivel chair, and he swiveled around to look out the window, like he's overlooking the Bay and not the parking lot. He was waiting for me to realize something just so he could swivel around when I did. I think that's probably what he does when we're not there. Practices his swiveling. I really had no choice. It was either look at the back of his head or the pile of junk. I went with the junk.*

Then I realized that this was no ordinary pile of junk. True, it could have been anyone's notebook, pencil, paper clips, gum, Life Savers, or Superman comic, but it wasn't just anyone's Dodgers cap, that's for sure. As you know, good buddy, there are only two in San Francisco, yours and mine, and since I had mine neatly jammed into my back pocket, this had to be yours.

And then I shuddered as I thought about you, out there, with no Dodgers cap.

Maly must have heard me gasp, or else he was just tired of pretending he wasn't looking at the parking lot. He swiveled around and took off his glasses. "Your friend Uchida forgot to clean out his locker. Would you like to be responsible for his belongings?" he asked.

I got the feeling that my other option was to be shipped overseas.

As soon as I uttered the magic word, "Sure," he said, "Good, good, good," and dove under his desk, reappearing with a small carton that he had

obviously placed there not wanting to waste time,
swept all your stuff into the carton, stood up, and
handed it to me, saying he appreciated my help
and I should please send his regards.

So I'm sending you Maly's regards and your
cap. The other junk I threw out. Are they stocking
any nice-sized trout in that lake of yours? Just re-
member to let the little ones go.

Robbie

Tuesday, July 21, 1942

Another letter from Robbie.

Ben —
Do you know how to write a letter? Do you know
how to write a postcard?

I mean, I appreciate getting your letter, but
maybe next time you could write more than four
sentences. You can do it, I know you can.

By the way, it sounds a bit crowded in that
apartment. Of course, it could be worse, you could
be bunking with Chuckeroo Hamada. Have you
seen him? Does he miss me?

Watch your back.

Robbie

Wednesday, July 22, 1942

Mrs. Shibutani came by today. I don't know why Mama is so nice to her. Aunt Mitsuko isn't. You can tell *she* doesn't like her. But Mama's never rude to anyone, even Mrs. Shibutani.

Mr. Shibutani's even worse. He's real creepy. I saw him yesterday smoking one of those big fat cigars he's always got clenched in his yellowing teeth. He was playing craps with a bunch of guys who looked even creepier than him. He was busy collecting money from them, and pouring something into a paper cup that they were passing around. Mr. Shibutani had a bottle behind his back, so probably that's what they were drinking.

Thursday, July 23, 1942

Last night the rain came down so hard, I thought the roof would cave in. It's the first time it's rained since we got here. It came suddenly, and sounded like it would last forever, which it has.

Now the place is one big mud puddle. There are planks all over and you're supposed to walk on them so you don't drown, but the water is so deep that half the planks are useless.

The mud is caked almost to the top of my shoes. I was

thinking I might borrow Mama's wooden clogs. Her *getas* are two or three inches high. Aunt Mitsuko's are even higher.

Friday, July 24, 1942

Mama got some material from Mrs. Watanabe and sewed curtains to replace the blankets. She said, "Don't you think they cheer the room up, Ben?" I didn't have the heart to say anything except, "They sure do, Mama."

Mama's trying to make the best of the situation, but frankly, curtains, blankets, it really doesn't make much difference to me. It's pretty ridiculous no matter how you look at it. Curtains don't change anything. The fact is we all have to live in this one stupid room with only pieces of cloth draped over the ropes to separate us. And the fact is that Papa's been taken somewhere and no one knows what's happening to him.

Last week, after Papa's letter came, it was like everyone was afraid to say what they were *really* thinking. The letter didn't sound like Papa *at all* — even the half of it that wasn't crossed out. All you could read was that he didn't want us to worry about him because he was "doing fine."

Mama doesn't want to talk about it. I asked her why Papa wasn't telling us what was happening to him. She said he would explain everything when he returned. When I talked to Naomi about it, she said we should just take care of things as best we can for as long as he's away.

I wanted to ask both of them why they were so sure he was coming back, but I didn't.

Saturday, July 26, 1942

There was a big crowd for today's opening game: nearly three thousand in attendance, someone said. It's because we're playing Block K. Everyone thinks we're going to be meeting again when we play for the championship. Mr. Tashima says there's lots of heavy betting going on. Gambling isn't really allowed, but everyone does it anyway. Mr. Tashima said that even the administration staff and soldiers are getting in on the action.

He brought Mama and Aunt Mitsuko, and the chairs that he made for our apartment. Most of the people had to stand.

Naomi got there early so she could draw Mike standing on the mound. When the game started, she went up on the roof of the ladies' latrine, which is down the first base line. She said she wanted to get a "bird's-eye view" for her sketch. I waved to her but she didn't see me. When Naomi's concentrating on her drawing, she doesn't see anything but what she's working on.

We won, three to two. It was a real squeaker, but Mike was flawless as usual. He pitched a two-hitter, and the two runs were unearned. He had his good stuff today. I knocked in two of the runs. I think it's because I got my cap back.

After the Boy Scouts finished playing "The Star-Spangled Banner," Josselit had to shake everyone's hand. I thought the game might be called on account of darkness, he was taking so long. Finally he actually got around to throwing out the first ball, which of course he threw about eight thousand feet above the catcher's head, nearly killing the right fielder's mother. As it turns out she just had a slight cut over her eye and was dizzy for a while.

But the two unearned runs came on an easy pop that the right fielder muffed because he was so worried about his poor mother, so, as far as I'm concerned, if it wasn't for Josselit, we would have had a shutout.

Tuesday, July 28, 1942

Mike wanted to work on his curve after school. Frankly, I don't know what he's worried about. When it comes in it looks like it fell off a table. No one can touch him when he's on.

After about an hour I told him I thought he should

give his arm a rest. He didn't think so. He's been in a pretty lousy mood lately. I think it's his parents. He has some pretty good battles with them. Sometimes when I come to get him, I can hear them before I'm halfway there. The first time I asked him what was going on. He just said he didn't like being told what to do and where to go.

If we run into them in the mess hall it's like Mike doesn't even see them. Once we were looking for a place to sit and there was room near them, but Mike said, "No way, they're jerks. Let's sit someplace else."

Wednesday, July 29, 1942

We played rock, paper, scissors, and watched Mr. Tashima play hearts. I never see him as happy as he is when he's playing hearts, except maybe when he's making something out of wood.

Mr. Tashima finished the medicine cabinet and hung it on the wall today. Now we can put our toothbrushes, toothpaste, and soap there. He also put up coat hooks and found a table lamp, so now I can write at night and not have to worry about waking everyone up.

friday, July 31, 1942

A letter from Robbie.

Ben —

By now you've probably heard the bad news about Pete crashing headfirst into the center-field wall, thanks to Enos Slaughter. Only Pete would have thrown the ball in to Pee Wee before collapsing. I hope I'm not the first one to tell you about this because I know he's your idol. I don't know how bad he's hurt — I think he has a concussion or something. I'm sure he'll be back in the lineup in no time flat, so don't worry.

This is going to be the Dodgers' big year no matter what. If it wasn't for Owen we would have won it all last year. Camilli's already having another MVP year, and he might end up with 30-plus HRs and 120 RBIs again. I told you Silly Philly was nuts to cough him up — he's worth every penny of the $45,000.

Now if only your boy Reiser can come back and hit .343 again, DiMaggio, here we come.

Hopefully they'll wrap this war stuff up real soon so that we can get on with the more important things in life, like the World Series. Speaking

*of important things, are you keeping your
promise? Not leaving anything out, are you?
Rumor is that Charles Hamada is there — are
you two roommates?*

Keep your eye on the ball.

Robbie

Saturday, August 1, 1942

Mama has decided to let Aunt Mitsuko cut my hair to
save money. She used to own her own beauty parlor, so
she knows how to cut hair. She already cuts Jimmy and
Mr. Tashima's hair and she's pretty good at it.

The barber down at the Wreck Hall is only 40
cents — half of what it was back home. But he doesn't do
such a good job and, anyway, the longer we're here and
the longer Mama doesn't hear from Papa, the more she
worries about money.

I asked Naomi if she thought we should go and talk to
Mama. Maybe that would help. Naomi didn't think that
was such a good idea. She's afraid it would upset Mama
more if we said something than if we just kept quiet. I
asked her if she thought we should write to Papa in that
place in Montana. But Naomi said she didn't think the
administration would let the letter out. There really isn't
anything to do but wait.

Monday, August 3, 1942

A package arrived today from Mr. Mills. He sent Mama the hot plate she asked for. Now she can make herself tea whenever she wants.

He says he hopes we are all well and that we shouldn't worry about our belongings because they're still safe and sound in his basement. Mama was relieved to hear this because some of the people in the camp have found out that their stuff has been stolen or destroyed. He asked if we had heard from Papa and, if we had, to please send his regards.

Tuesday, August 4, 1942

Mama, Naomi, and Aunt Mitsuko were laughing so loud when they came back from the laundry that they woke me up. Usually the racket from Jimmy's wagon — that's what they use to cart the laundry back and forth — makes enough noise by itself, but this time it was them.

They were talking about when Aunt Mitsuko first came to America for her arranged marriage. She was a picture bride just like Mama. The only difference is that when Aunt Mitsuko arrived and met her husband-to-be, he was much older than the picture he sent. And, as it turned out, that wasn't the only lie he told. He wasn't *really* the president of a railroad, like he had written. He was just another Japanese laying the tracks.

Aunt Mitsuko said she came to America to get rich, and so she decided to go off on her own, and that's what they were laughing about, which doesn't sound so funny to me.

Mama spends more time at the laundry than she does in the apartment. The U.S. may be at war with Japan, but Mama has declared war on dirt. For Mama, every day is wash day. Frankly, I think the three of them are having a little too much fun over there. They're always laughing or yakking away when they come back from the laundry.

I did find out where my jeans were, though. Mama took them. I wish she would let me wear them to school, but she won't listen to a word about it. There's a big meeting next week to decide if we can wear jeans and if the girls can wear pants. Mama doesn't care about the meeting. And she doesn't care what anyone decides. As far as she is concerned, all the kids here are getting *waga-mama*, and she says she doesn't want me to get spoiled, too.

I asked her how come Mike can wear jeans to class. Mama didn't even answer me. She never answers questions like that. I wish Papa were here. He's more reasonable about things like this.

Tuesday, August 4, 1942

Miss Kroll announced the decision on dress regulations. They decided to leave it up to the teachers. Not much of a decision, if you ask me. Miss Kroll said she had given the matter a lot of thought. When someone says that, you know they haven't given it any thought and just decided what they were going to do about two seconds ago. Anyway, she decided that we could wear whatever we wanted — including jeans — under one condition. I couldn't wait to hear what the one condition was.

We could wear whatever we wanted if *everyone* handed in their completed homework assignment *on time every day*. Especially "those of you who haven't been handing in your homework at all." She was walking up and down the narrow aisles between the benches, and just as she was saying the last part she stopped right in front of me and looked down. After class I went up to her and said, "Miss Kroll, let me see if I got this right. Are you saying that if I don't start doing my homework you're going to make everyone dress up and then tell them I'm to blame?"

She was marking some papers, and when she looked up, she took off her glasses. I never realized that her lips were so puffy. Actually, I had never really been that close to Miss Kroll. I could even smell her perfume. I was going to step back but I didn't want her to think I was scared.

She stuck her pencil in her hair — for safekeeping, I guess — and looked at me for the longest time. She looked like she was going to say something real nice, so I wasn't at all prepared for what she *did* say: "You're a real disappointment, Ben." Then she put her glasses back on, took her pencil out of her hair, and went back to working on her papers. I thought that was really unnecessary, if you want to know the truth.

Saturday, August 8, 1942

Mrs. Watanabe brought some flowers she had grown, and Mama arranged them in the vase that Aunt Mitsuko made in ceramics class. She also brought radishes, green onions, lettuce, and carrots from her garden. I'm not real big on carrots, but after all the garbage I get to eat here, at least her carrots tasted like carrots. Jimmy had to have one as soon as he saw mine. Now he's a big carrot fan.

Mrs. Watanabe looks like she's going to have her baby real soon.

Monday, August 10, 1942

Sunday, after practice, me, Mike, and Kenny went over to the Wreck Hall to watch this week's movie. The line was all the way down to the post office, so by the time we got in, it had already started.

The movie was Abbott and Costello in *Hold That Ghost*, which wasn't worth the dime I had to borrow from Naomi. The only places to sit were in the front row. We had to sit on the floor and tilt our heads way back so we could see the movie. It was a real pain in the neck. Ha ha.

You couldn't watch the movie even if you wanted to. People were talking, moving around trying to get a better seat, or going in and out, with their kids stepping on your hands half the time. Some of the *Issei* even take off their shoes while they watch, which made me feel like puking.

Kenny fell asleep five seconds after we sat down, and Mike said he was so bored he was going back to his apartment to go to sleep. I stayed. I like to see a movie until the end — even if it's an Abbott and Costello movie.

I took my time walking back. There are no streetlights and I didn't want to fall into a ditch or run into a wall. On the way, I saw Mike talking to Mr. Shibutani, which was odd. First of all, I don't know how Mike would know a guy like Mr. Shibutani and, even if he did, why would he be talking to him? They were standing in the doorway of Mr. Shibutani's apartment. He is always hanging around there smoking cigars with his friends, who look as creepy as he does.

I just watched for a while. I mean, it wasn't like I was in a hurry to get anywhere. The conversation looked pretty serious, and Mr. Shibutani kept puffing on his cigar and blowing smoke right in Mike's face. Then they both started laughing. I thought Mr. Shibutani must have told a good joke or something. After they finished laughing, they shook hands and Mr. Shibutani patted Mike on the back like he was congratulating him for something.

At first I was going to wait in the road and ask him what the joke was about, but I thought the better of it and stood against the barracks, hiding in the darkness as he walked by. Then today I asked him what Mr. Shibutani said that was so funny. He looked right past me, like he didn't want to look me in the eye. "I don't know what you're talking about," he said. I tried to remind him about the serious conversation, the big joke, the cigar, everything. He said he didn't know anyone named Shibutani. Maybe it wasn't him. Maybe I'm wrong. It sure looked like him, though.

Thursday, August 13, 1942

Even though he doesn't have to, Charles still wears a suit every single day. I would die if I had to wear a suit.

He hasn't been in school all week, which is not like Charles. He thinks attendance is an actual subject — something he should excel in. I asked him where he's been. He said his parents were concerned because one of the girls in our class went to the hospital. They say now she has polio. Polio's like leprosy around here. If you want some peace and quiet all you have to do is say, "I think I'm coming down with a bad case of polio," and watch 'em run.

Friday, August 14, 1942

The new blackboards were delivered today. They're not exactly black, though. They're red. They're plywood that's been painted red, so it's hard to think of them as blackboards. But since Miss Kroll would like us to, I'll try my best.

Monday, August 15, 1942

Me, Mike, and Kenny eat together now because we have practice every night. Mama isn't exactly thrilled, but she has kind of given up. Plus I think she's more upset about the letter from Papa than anything else. She didn't let me or Naomi read it. All she said is that Papa is "doing fine" and hopes to join us soon. I wanted to say something to Mama but I could see that Naomi didn't want me to. Maybe she's right.

Tuesday, August 18, 1942

We played splits after practice. We had to go where no one could see us because if they knew Mike had a knife, we would be in serious trouble.

Kenny didn't know how to play, so we showed him how you throw the knife so that it sticks in the ground far enough away from the other guy that he has to stretch his leg to reach the knife blade. You play until one guy can't stretch anymore, splits his pants, or falls down.

On Mike's third throw, when Kenny was really stretched pretty far already, he stuck the knife blade right into Kenny's ankle. Kenny let out a pretty loud scream, but luckily no one heard it. He realized real quick that if anyone *did* hear us we would all be dead by morning, so he shut up. He made all kinds of awful faces while I pulled out the knife, but no noise.

Mike didn't even look like he felt bad. He didn't say anything to Kenny, and I had to make him help me get

Kenny back to the barracks. I couldn't think of anyplace else to take him.

Naomi was there, which was lucky because you can always count on her in situations like this. She examined Kenny's foot and told me to get some hot, soapy water from the mess hall. Then she cleaned the cut and wrapped it tightly in a towel. She told Kenny to lie down until the bleeding stopped and after that to keep it clean and try to stay off it as much as possible.

Naomi said the cut wasn't deep and he had a fifty-fifty chance of living. Kenny tried to laugh but it hurt too much. The strange thing was Mike. All of a sudden he wasn't there. He didn't look at Naomi once, and then before I knew it, he was gone.

Wednesday, August 19, 1942

Naomi didn't come home until late last night because she was finishing her drawings for the first edition of the *Mirror Lake Free Press*. Now that takes real guts, naming a newspaper at a prison camp the *Free Press*. The only thing about it that's free is the cost, and frankly, I think they're overcharging. It's just like a regular newspaper only it doesn't have any travel advertisements.

Wednesday, August 26, 1942

Mama's wearing pants. It's the first time I've ever seen her in anything but a dress. I asked her if the *Free Press* was sending over a reporter to do a fashion article on her, but she didn't think that was funny.

I thought Mama would never give in, but everyone wears pants now, even *Issei* like Mama. It's just too windy and dusty, and dresses go flying all over the place. Aunt Mitsuko ordered the pants from Sears, the mail-order place. They came yesterday and Aunt Mitsuko had to wait in line for an hour and a half at the post office. Everyone's starting to get their clothes from Sears. You can't exactly go shopping around here. If it keeps up like this, everyone is going to look exactly alike.

Mama looked embarrassed at first, but Naomi's got the same exact pair and Mr. Tashima said they looked like sisters. Mama's been strutting around ever since she heard that. They do look alike, I have to admit, but *sisters?* I don't know about Mr. Tashima sometimes.

Thursday, August 27, 1942

I can't believe Charles Hamada has to sit in the front row, just like he did back home. I don't know what he's trying to prove. He's still the world's biggest brownnose. Every time Miss Kroll asks one of her lame questions, his arm shoots straight up in the air. Sometimes I think it's going to come right out of its socket and become permanently stuck in the ceiling. If Charles isn't called on right away, he starts jiggling his hand and making funny sounds.

I think Miss Kroll hates Charles about as much as I do. Most of the time she doesn't call on him, even when he's the only one raising his hand. I'm not a hundred percent sure, but I think I can see her smile when she ignores him like that.

Monday, August 31, 1942

Miss Kroll said that the books should be here by next week, but she says that every week.

Tuesday, September 1, 1942

Charles has been coming around too much. He's so annoying, even Naomi can't stand it. I had to come up with something, and it was no use trying to hint — it just goes right over Charles's head. I wracked my brains thinking of a good way to tell him to get lost. Mike said I should place a notice in the camp newspaper. He's a real help.

I was about to give up and just face the fact that I have

to spend the rest of the war with Charles Hamada —
truly a fate worse than death — or, if not, surely more
boring than death — when it came to me. It was, if I may
say so myself, one of my more brilliant ideas. I had Naomi
paint an official-looking sign that said QUARANTINED and
then I put it up outside our barracks. By the time I went
to school this morning I had forgotten about it.

Charles kept looking at me like I was a Martian or
something. He was so stunned seeing me that he didn't
even raise his hand once.

At lunch I went over to him, but he backed away. I
asked him what was wrong, but he put up his hand and
told me not to come any closer. I said, okay, but only if he
would tell me what was going on. He asked me how I was
feeling. I told him I was feeling fine. He asked if it was
okay for me to be out of quarantine. I almost laughed, but
caught myself. I put on a very serious face and told him
the doctors thought the contagious period had passed
and it was okay for me to go to school, but I had to come
right home after and be sure not to touch anyone, just to
be on the safe side.

Charles said he had to go.

Thursday, September 3, 1942

Mike wanted me and Kenny to come with him and sneak into the residence area today. That's where Josselit, Miss Kroll, the other teachers, and all the Caucasians in the administration live. It's strictly off-limits, but Mike said there would be no one around because they were having some kind of big-deal meeting.

I didn't want him to think I was chicken but I didn't want to be gunned down in the prime of my life by some trigger-happy MP either. I told him I didn't think it was such a good idea and Kenny chipped in with "Me, too." That didn't exactly sit well with him. Mike likes to have things his way.

Kenny didn't say anything. They've been staying away from each other since the knife-throwing incident.

Friday, September 4, 1942

Mike got in last night and no one caught him. He said their barracks are all painted on the inside and there's indoor toilets and showers and refrigerators and all kinds of food and stuff we don't have. He's planning to go back and take what he can.

Saturday, September 5, 1942

Mama made me help her hang the wash on the outdoor clotheslines. Usually Naomi helps her with that kind of junk, but Mama said she was drawing something for the newspaper. As if that's a better excuse than baseball practice.

There are about a million clotheslines strung up around here. You've got to watch your step or you can accidentally hang yourself on your own underwear.

Tuesday, September 8, 1942

School is so stupid, even Miss Kroll looks bored. She doesn't even ask me about my homework anymore. I knew she'd see things my way after a while. I wish Mike and Kenny were in my class but they're a grade ahead of me. Mike sits in the back of his class just like me. We both sit right near the partition, so we agreed he would tap 3-2-2-3 to signal me. I can hear him if I lean back and put my head against the wall.

I didn't think anyone would notice, but Miss Kroll asked me, right in front of everyone, if I felt the work here in the seventh grade wasn't challenging enough. She thought I seemed to be paying more attention to what was going on in the eighth grade.

It was kind of embarrassing because at the exact moment that everyone turned around to look at me, I lost my balance and crashed to the floor. You could see that Miss Kroll thought I did it on purpose, which isn't true at all, but there was no way I was going to convince her of that.

Mike said the crash was so loud that everyone in his class cracked up also. I hope this doesn't spoil my chances of getting into Mirror Lake University.

Sunday, September 13, 1942

Mrs. Watanabe had her baby yesterday. She's coming back from the hospital tomorrow.

Wednesday, September 16, 1942

Mama said Mrs. Watanabe's baby sleeps in the top drawer of the dresser because there is no better place. Mama's eyes were all watery when she told me.

She also said that Mr. Watanabe is upset that he will never have any baby pictures of his son because no one is allowed to have a camera here. I wonder what it's going to be like when the baby grows up and someone asks him, "Hey, where were you born?" Will he have to say "the Mirror Lake Prison Camp"?

Sunday, September 20, 1942

Mr. Tashima spends all his time now working on the new school they're building. Yesterday morning they poured the concrete for the sidewalk leading up to the front door, even though there isn't a front door yet. He took me down with him so I could write my name in the wet concrete. It looks swell.

Mama thinks it's good news that they're building a school, but I don't think she realizes that means we're going to be here for a while.

Mr. Tashima even has identification papers so that he can go into town with Mr. Watanabe and the rest of his crew and get building materials. Town is only an hour away. I asked him why he didn't just run away once he was there. He could be a free man and no one would be able to find him.

At first he smiled and said that his face just might give him away. But then he looked troubled and said, "What would happen to my sister and my son if I left them, and how would I find my wife and daughter?" I guess I didn't think of that. And besides, I had completely forgotten about Mrs. Tashima and Jimmy's sister.

Aunt Mitsuko goes to the post office every day to see if there's a letter from them and every day she comes home empty-handed. The first few weeks, Mr. Tashima used to always make sure he was around when she came back. The look on his face when he realized there was nothing was terrible to see. But after a while, he didn't even wait around, just went about doing whatever it was he was doing. That's why I forgot, even though she still goes, every day.

I hope Mr. Tashima isn't mad at me for reminding him.

Monday. September 21. 1942

Mr. Tashima asked me to help him because he's so busy working on the new school building and being block manager. I was so glad he was talking to me the same as he usually does that I would have done anything, except maybe clean out the men's latrine.

He wants me to hand out the latest list of rules and regulations from the administration. I have to put one up in every apartment and tack one up in Wreck Hall, the mess hall, the canteen, the latrine, and the laundry room.

1) ALL PERSONS OF JAPANESE
ANCESTRY SHALL REMAIN WITHIN
THEIR PLACE OF RESIDENCE BETWEEN
THE HOURS OF 7 p.m. and 6:00 a.m.
UNLESS OTHERWISE DIRECTED BY THE
MILITARY. THIS DOES NOT INCLUDE
ACCESS TO THE LAUNDRY AND LAVATORY
FACILITIES.
2) THERE WILL BE NO MEETING OR
GATHERING WITHOUT MILITARY
APPROVAL.
3) THERE WILL BE NO INCOMING
OR OUTGOING TELEPHONE OR TELEGRAPH
MESSAGES WITHOUT MILITARY
APPROVAL.
4) FAILURE TO OBSERVE THE
RULES WILL RESULT IN STRICT
DISCIPLINARY ACTION.

R.R. Josselit
Project Director

Tuesday, September 22, 1942

Someone snuck into Wreck Hall last night and wrote PRISON SCHOOL about a million times in bright red paint all over the wall. The teachers have worked themselves into a real uproar about it. It's the only thing they talked about today, whispering to each other, cupping their hands over their mouths so we can't see what they're saying. They're *dying* to know who did it. Me, too.

Miss Kroll announced that Mr. Josselit is coming tomorrow to give us a big speech about "the incident." I can't wait for that.

Wednesday, September 23, 1942

The speech wasn't very long. It was pretty standard: "having respect for public property," "acting in a civilized manner," and some real funny stuff about how his door is always open for those of us "who wish to voice our feelings in a civilized manner." I guess he doesn't think writing Prison School all over in red paint is mature.

How could anyone who is in charge of thousands of people who are being held prisoner talk about acting "in a civilized manner?" And as far as this open-door policy is concerned, yeah, his door is open *if* you can get past the two MPs who guard it twenty-four hours a day. I mean, who's kidding who here? I think his speech was so short because it was right before lunch and he was hungry.

Thursday, September 24, 1942

Mama's mad at me because I didn't take a shower. I just don't think it's worth it. If I have to stand in line for *one more thing* I'm going to jump out of my skin. That's all I ever do around here. I have to stand in line to brush my teeth, eat my food, and go to the bathroom. I DON'T WANT TO STAND IN LINE FOR ANYTHING ELSE. Besides, there's never any hot water and I feel like a fool taking a shower with the entire Japanese population of the United States.

Naomi won't even *go* there anymore. Last week someone took her bathrobe while she was taking a shower. That was it for her. She said she would wash after the war.

I agreed to take a shower once a week, but I'm only going late at night. That's the only time you're likely to get any hot water and be left alone.

Friday, September 25, 1942

It was really, really cold last night. The frost killed most of Mrs. Watanabe's garden. Her new baby cried all night. You could hear him from one end of the block to the other. This morning when Mr. Watanabe came to get Mr. Tashima, he looked real tired. He told Mr. Tashima that he was up half the night walking around with the baby.

Sunday, September 27, 1942

Kenny hit a home run over the left-field fence today so the game had to be called after only four innings. That's one of the things that's different about baseball here. If someone hits a home run to left, you can't go get the ball. If you do you might get machine-gunned to death by one of those itchy-fingered guards who might think you're trying to make an escape.

Usually we have extra balls, but not today.

Monday, September 28, 1942

The latest edition of the camp newspaper is hot off the presses. After reading it, I think Robbie may be right. I just might be at a resort. The only good thing about the paper is Naomi's drawings. The one she did of Mike on the mound was in this issue. I told her it was one of her best but she just said, "It's okay." I don't know what's going on there, but it isn't good.

THE MIRROR LAKE FREE PRESS
NOTICE OF UPCOMING EVENTS

»THURSDAY OCTOBER 1: There will be a concert by THE MIRROR LAKE JAZZ BAND at the recreation hall.
   The show begins promptly at 7:00 p.m. Tickets are now on sale at the canteen. ADULTS 20¢ and CHILDREN 10¢

»FRIDAY OCTOBER 2: FRIDAY NIGHT HOP
   Just arrived new recordings

BALLET AND INTERPRETIVE DANCE CLASSES will meet at 2:00 p.m. Saturdays. Anyone interested see MISS KROLL to sign up.

SPECIAL REMINDERS:
   *Don't forget the TALENT SHOW Saturday, OCTOBER 10.
   *AUDITIONS will be run until Wednesday, noon. NO APPLICATIONS AFTER THAT.
   *Be smart: Be early

SATURDAY BASEBALL:
Block B (7-0) V.
Block M (2-5)
  1:00 P.M. GAME TIME

*SIGN UP FOR NEW CLASSES: Flower
arranging, sewing, doll making

*NEXT WEEK'S FEATURE ARTICLES:
  *Ten steps to fire safety
  *How to get your marriage licence

Tuesday, September 29, 1942

Mr. Tashima and Aunt Mitsuko were arguing about something again last night. They don't like anyone to hear, so
they went for a walk. But when they came back, I heard
Mr. Tashima say *oso katta* to Aunt Mitsuko, which means
"it's too late." But too late for what, I don't know.

There have been many meetings recently, and Mr.
Tashima comes home late almost every night.

Monday, October 5, 1942

After practice Kenny said he had something to show me. He looked really excited, but wouldn't tell me what it was until we got there. There turned out to be this building behind Wreck Hall where they stash all those empty cartons and surplus stuff they don't know what to do with.

We had to put two really tall, rickety ladders up against the wall and climb up about a zillion feet. We were so high up that my head was almost hitting the ceiling. Kenny pointed to a hole in the wall and told me to look through it. All I saw was a room just like the one we were in, except it didn't have any of the cartons and junk that this one did.

After a minute or two I heard something, and then saw about a thousand Camp Fire girls filing in and lining up like they were going to do some kind of dance, which they were. They were rehearsing for the talent show next week. "They're going to wear costumes," Kenny said, like he had deciphered some secret code or something. At first I thought, *Who cares what they're going to wear*, but then the light went on. Kenny had discovered the room where the Camp Fire girls were going to change into their costumes. Change as in naked.

Now I was as excited as Kenny, and said I would tell

Mike and we would all meet back here next week, right before the talent show. "No," Kenny said, "don't tell him."

I couldn't believe what I was hearing. Kenny never said anything bad about *anyone*. Never. He even talks to Charles Hamada, and no one ever does that. He and Mike always got along, at least until Mike stuck the knife in Kenny's ankle. Maybe that was it. "What are you talking about?" I asked.

"Never mind, just don't tell him. I don't trust him and that's all," Kenny said. Kenny is really easygoing and he doesn't put his foot down often. When he does you know that's it, so I just said, "Okay, if that's the way you want it." He said that it was.

Tuesday, October 6, 1942

This week's camp newspaper is even more full of it than usual. It's got an article about how great the administration is and what a good job they're doing. There's a list of improvements they've made and are planning to make. They say we should all look on the bright side.

I asked Naomi why they wrote all this stuff, and she said that if they don't write articles that praise the administration and the project director, they'll just shut down the newspaper. That's democracy at work.

All during practice I wondered if Mike could tell that I was keeping something from him. He didn't seem to notice, but you never know with him.

Friday, October 9, 1942

Aunt Mitsuko and Mama worked on their English homework together last night. They didn't even go to dinner. I must say, they're getting pretty good. You can almost understand Aunt Mitsuko when she speaks English now.

Mama's afraid to make a mistake, but she works real hard. She practices her pronunciation and writing every night, no matter what. I told her she's a good student. She said it's too bad it doesn't run in the family. Very funny.

Saturday, October 10, 1942

I had to go to the library so I could get the newspaper and see how the Dodgers were doing. The *Free Press* doesn't exactly have a great sports page, although they did do a big spread on our upcoming championship game against Block K next week.

Sunday, October 11, 1942

There was only one problem with Kenny's talent show idea. There wasn't anything to see.

The Camp Fire girls were there, all right, but they had their costumes on by the time they arrived. Obviously, they had changed somewhere else. They just stood around in little groups, looking giddy and nervous and practicing these stupid dance routines. The most they were doing was fixing their hair.

Tuesday, October 13, 1942

A letter from Robbie.

> Ben —
>
> I don't know who had a worse year, you or the Dodgers. I thought you had it locked. Of course, I thought they had it locked.
>
> I mean, Ben, we had a 10 1/2 game lead on August 15th. 10 1/2 games. Who would have thought Cooper would win 22? And by the way, did you catch that stunt where he changed his uniform for every game he pitched? Wearing jersey #19 when he was going for victory #19 and jersey #20 when he was going for #20 all the way to #22. What a jerk.

And who would have thought the Cards would win 43 out of the last 51? 21 out of the 26 in September? 21 out of 26! But that's what I like about the Dodgers — they always find a way to lose.

Speaking of losing, I think we've got the inside track to a losing season this year. It just ain't the same without you. No one, not even Reiser, can play center like you, and you'll never guess who took your place. Donny Moody. Not only is he playing center — or should I say standing in center — but coach has him batting third. Believe me, it's hopeless. Maybe you could tell them you're vital to the war effort — my war effort.

And speaking of hopeless, I've just about given up any hope of getting a letter from you. I know you're really pressed for time but give it a shot. And remember, as the Dodgers surely will,

Expect the unexpected.

Robbie

Monday, October 19, 1942

"Expect the unexpected" — Motto Man sure got that one right. Saturday, October 17, 1942. A day — in the words of our beloved President — that will live in infamy. My personal infamy.

It all began in the eighth inning of the championship game against Block K. A leadoff double, two singles, a home run and, just like that, we were behind 4–2. I thought the inning would never end.

In the top of the ninth, Kenny and Ricky got on. I was up with men on first and second, two outs. The first pitch was high and outside, but the ump called it a strike. I fouled off the next one, bringing the count to 0 and 2.

When I stepped out of the batter's box, I noticed that the right fielder was playing way over toward center. I bat righty so he must have figured it was a safe bet. *I* figured he was making a big mistake and if I waited on the ball I could prove it to him in a way that he would never forget.

The next one was in the dirt a foot in front of the plate. It got by the catcher, but not quite far enough for Kenny or Ricky to advance. I knew he wasn't going to risk another one in the dirt. He was going to come right in with the next pitch.

I nailed it — I could tell by the right fielder's stunned look as the ball fell just inside the foul line. I was flying by the time I rounded second. I could see Kenny crossing the plate and Ricky right behind him. The score was tied. Time to gamble.

Mr. Wakasa, the third-base coach, was signaling me to slow down — I had third standing up. It never crossed his mind that I wasn't going to stop at third.

By now the catcher had figured out what was going on and had taken off his mask. He was giving me that "who do you think you are" look. He was the one who hit the home run, and he thought he was a real big deal. That's what made me decide not to slide — I just ran him over instead. We both had to be helped up, but I was safe. We were ahead 5–4.

The next batter grounded out. Bottom of the ninth. Three outs away from the championship. I should have seen it coming. But I wanted to believe that Mike was just having a bad day and now that we were ahead, he would settle down and be his old self.

Mike's first pitch was lined right past third for a stand-up double. The next batter singled to left. Man on first and third, no outs. I'd never seen Mike pitch this bad. Never. He was hurrying every pitch. As soon as the guy stepped into the batter's box he went into his windup. It was like he didn't care if the guy hit it or not. Like he didn't care if we won or lost.

He *didn't* care if the guy hit it or not. He *didn't* care if we won or lost. All the pieces started to fit together. Why Kenny didn't trust Mike. That night with Mr. Shibutani and him saying I must have seen someone else. The way he acted sometimes.

He walked the next two guys, and just like that the

game was tied. I waved my arms as I ran in, hoping the ump would see me in time. When I got to the mound, I said, "What do you think you're doing?" He didn't even have the guts to look at me — just like he didn't the day I asked him about Mr. Shibutani. He was looking down, concentrating on digging at the dirt with the heel of his shoe.

I stood there, waiting. I wanted to hear what he had to say. I wanted to hear if he had a good explanation for what was going on. "Just go play your position, Uchida," he said, still not looking at me. I was about to punch his face in when the ump hollered, "Let's get going, boys."

The rest is all a blur. Mike ended up hitting a batter right in the middle of the back, walking in the winning run. I remember running in from center field, hoping I could get in enough good shots before anyone pulled me off. But someone beat me to it. By the time they got Kenny off Mike he was cut up pretty bad. His right eye was already starting to close and blood was trickling from the corner of his mouth.

No one said anything on the way home. I could see that Naomi wanted to but she didn't. I didn't really feel like talking about it to anyone, except maybe Robbie and he wasn't around.

Thursday, October 22, 1942

Kenny and me saw Mike at dinner. I'm not sure if he saw us. His right eye looks real bad. I heard he might not be able to see out of it. Ever. Kenny didn't even look at him. He's still boiling mad.

There's talk all over camp. Everyone says he threw the game, and call him *akuto*. They say he's in with Shibutani and his crowd and there was lots of money riding on the game and they paid Mike off.

I still have a hard time believing all this, but as Motto Man would say, "Money makes the world go round."

Sunday, October 25, 1942

Everyone has been on edge since the shooting. All anyone knows for sure is that Mr. Watanabe was driving one of Mr. Tashima's trucks when it happened. He had picked up a load of lumber for the new school and got a flat tire. By the time he got back to camp it was real late. He was stopped by one of the MPs. There were shots and they found Mr. Watanabe lying on the ground, dead.

Mama has been with Mrs. Watanabe since Friday. Naomi is there, too, helping with the baby.

Tuesday, October 27, 1942

Each day there are more stories about what happened. Some people say the administration didn't like Mr. Watanabe because his speeches stirred up the people. They considered him a troublemaker, so they had him killed.

Naomi heard that the MP had it in for all the Japanese in the camp because his brother was killed in the attack on Pearl Harbor. Mr. Watanabe was just in the wrong place at the wrong time.

Mr. Tashima has been silent. Mama says he feels responsible for Mr. Watanabe's death. Today was the first day I had the courage to ask him about it. Mr. Tashima's generally a pretty soft-spoken guy, but he spoke even softer than usual. He said Mr. Watanabe wasn't really a troublemaker. He was just a good worker who wanted the administration to do something about some of the bad conditions in the camp. I wanted to ask him if he thought the MP was told to kill Mr. Watanabe, but then I decided it wasn't such a good idea.

Wednesday, October 28, 1942

Mr. Tashima is worried that everyone is so mad about the killing that something bad could happen. I heard him talking to some men last night. They were talking low, but I could hear most of what they said. The men wanted to burn down the administration building in retaliation. They were going to put straw-filled mattresses under the building, soak them with oil, and set them on fire.

Mr. Tashima tried to calm them down, which wasn't exactly easy. He said there was no proof that the shooting wasn't an accident. He said everyone should wait until the facts come out. The men laughed when he said that, and then they walked out, slamming the door behind them and waking up Jimmy.

Mr. Tashima sat up with Jimmy till he went back to sleep. Then he paced up and down. I could hear Aunt Mitsuko trying to convince him to get some sleep, but he just walked around all night looking out the window like he was expecting the whole place to go up in flames any minute. Maybe he knows something I don't.

Thursday, October 29, 1942

There was an article in the camp newspaper that said a review board was going to make a "full inquiry" into the recent "incident" involving Mr. Watanabe. That's what they called it, an "incident." The guy's dead as a doornail and they call it an incident. I wonder what they would call the Civil War, a disturbance?

There are only Caucasians on the review board, so nobody expects much.

Monday, November 2, 1942

Tomorrow the review board is going to announce their findings. I bet they find that Mr. Watanabe is still dead.

Tuesday, November 3, 1942

Josselit announced the review board's decision. They said that Mr. Watanabe was intoxicated and insulted the MP and threatened him with violence. The MP, they concluded, had no choice but to shoot Mr. Watanabe in self-defense.

That's a good one, Mr. Watanabe — all five feet three inches of him — threatening a two-hundred-pound MP holding a semiautomatic rifle. The MP was being charged with "misuse of government property" and was to pay a fifty-cent fine for the bullets. That'll teach him.

Some of the people booed and threw things at him. You could tell that Josselit was put out by everyone's behavior because he kept wiping his forehead with his stupid handkerchief, even though it wasn't that hot. He spoke through a loudspeaker and his voice was booming. He warned everyone to be calm and remain in their seats, but no one paid much attention. The aisles were filled with people yelling things and waving their arms. Finally he announced that he had no choice — he was calling in the MPs to restore order.

The MPs came running in like they were taking an enemy beachhead and scrambled down the aisles, pushing people with their rifles and herding them back into their seats. I never saw most of these guys before, and there sure were a lot of them. Josselit must have sent for reinforcements as soon as he knew the review board's finding wasn't going to be a real crowd pleaser.

The Head MP took the microphone away from Josselit — who looked like he was holding a live grenade and was greatly relieved to have someone else take over — and announced that everyone had to be back in their barracks in ten minutes. Some of the MPs looked like they were in the mood for some target practice, so we all scurried back to our apartments.

I thought for sure I would see Mike there — I mean practically everyone in the entire camp was there. I didn't see him and I didn't see his pal Shibutani. They were probably sitting around cooking up their next scam. Kenny said that Ricky heard that Mike and his father had one of their arguments last week and Mike moved in with Mr. Shibutani.

Friday, November 6, 1942

I've decided to hide my journal. Things are just a little too crazy around here since Mr. Watanabe was killed. I've been keeping it under the bed, but that's no good. There's a crawl space under the barracks that's just big enough for me to get in and out. I don't think a grown-up could get in, and if they did they probably couldn't get out.

Mama still spends most of the day with Mrs. Watanabe. Naomi says Mama is not able to get her to eat anything yet.

Thursday, November 12, 1942

Jimmy asked me to take him to the Bird Man yesterday. The guy's a little cuckoo, if you ask me. They say that back home he was a music teacher.

No one knows where he got those two little birds. They were just babies when he found them. In the beginning he fed them crumbled up cookies, but now he's got all the kids in the camp catching worms and insects and bringing them to him.

Jimmy loves to go over there and see their trick. As soon as the birds see the Bird Man give Jimmy the cookie to hold between his lips, they start cocking their heads this way and that and looking all over the place with their beady little eyes.

They live in a beautiful bird cage that Mr. Tashima made for them. But the Bird Man never closes the doors so they come and go as they please. They fly out, swoop around like attack fighters, and land on top of Jimmy's head. One waits there while the other flutters in front of Jimmy's face, taking teeny-weeny bird bites out of the cookie. Jimmy's a real favorite with the birds because he doesn't laugh and drop the cookie like the other kids. He stands straight and doesn't move a muscle. The only thing he does is he keeps his eyes closed the whole time because the fast fluttering of their little wings scares the devil out of him.

The Bird Man's apartment is right next door to Mr. Shibutani's, so I was ready to run into him or Mike. Luckily I didn't.

Saturday, November 14, 1942

Me, Jimmy, and Kenny played marbles all morning. Kenny brought them from home, which was a smart move on his part. After that we went to play kick-the-can. On the way we saw a whole bunch of empty cartons behind Wreck Hall. We piled them up and made a really big fort and played the Alamo. I was Davy Crockett and Kenny and Jimmy were Mexicans.

I must admit this is a great place to play kick-the-can. I mean, nothing gets in your way. No cars, no curbs, no trees, nothing. Just miles and miles of dirt and desolation. You could kick-the-can until you kicked the bucket. Of course it's a high price to pay — I mean coming here — just to play a great game of kick-the-can.

Tuesday, November 17, 1942

Mama didn't get a copy of the camp newspaper this week. There was a paper shortage, so they ran out. She really looks forward to it. She reads all the stupid local news and the Japanese page. Naomi said she might be able to find a copy when she goes to the office tomorrow night. Naomi's got connections.

Aunt Mitsuko yelled at the girl in the barracks next door because she plays her radio full blast all day and doesn't even turn it down at night. I don't think the girl understood a word Aunt Mitsuko said, though, because she was speaking Japanese.

Wednesday, November 18, 1942

There's an article in this week's *Free Press* about how much better and easier it is now that they've put in street signs and streetlights.

They named each street after a different tree: Maple, Walnut, Birch, Tulip. Since there aren't any trees, it might have made more sense if they'd named the streets after things we see every day: Machine Gun Lane, Barbed Wire Boulevard, Electric Fence Avenue — things like that.

I must admit that the streetlights *are* good because now you can actually see where you're going at night. Of course they don't mention how many times we've all come close to killing ourselves walking around in the dark for the past six months.

Friday, November 20, 1942

I couldn't get to sleep last night. If it wasn't the searchlights shining through the window every fifteen minutes, it was the mice. Or at least I think they're mice.

I figured I would go outside, sit on the bench, and look at the stars for a while. It reminded me of last summer, when Papa showed me the stars with his new telescope. He told me that they really aren't stars at all, that each one of those stars is really a sun, just like ours. They just twinkle like that because they are so far away.

Papa said that each one of those suns has lots of planets circling around it, just like the earth circles our sun. He said there is even a good chance that somewhere out there, there's a planet just like ours, and that there's someone just like me looking up at the stars and wondering if there's someone just like him.

It made me wish Papa was looking up at the same stars and thinking about me as much as I'm thinking about him.

Sunday, November 22, 1942

Naomi was crying when I got home. Some of the little girls next door were playing house, she said. They were standing in line holding up their empty plates, and Naomi asked them what they were doing. They said they were waiting for their dinners. I didn't see what was so bad about that, and I could see that Naomi was getting mad at me because I didn't get it.

"Don't you see," she said, practically screaming at me. "These little girls are growing up thinking that standing in line with a tray in a mess hall is the way it's supposed to be. They don't even know about setting your own table or sitting down to eat in your own kitchen with just your family. They're not going to know that this way isn't right. What's going to happen to them? What's going to happen to us?" Then she hid her face in her hands and started to cry even worse than before.

I didn't know what to say, so I said the truth. Papa always said the truth is always the best solution. So I said, "That's a good question," and, for some strange reason, it made Naomi laugh, although she didn't stop crying completely.

That night, when I came back from the movie, I decided to sit on the bench for a while. I just didn't feel like going inside.

The movie was interesting. It made me think about stuff. It was about this kid named Charles Foster Kane who was being given up by his mama because his father hit him and she wanted to get him away from all that. His mama had been left a lot of money by one of her boarders: She ran a boardinghouse.

You could see that giving him up was something the mama didn't want to do. She was doing it for her son's sake — so he would have a better life. She turns him over to this lawyer, who becomes the kid's guardian.

When the boy grows up and his parents are dead, he's really, really rich. He uses the money to buy himself a newspaper. He becomes a very powerful man and has a couple of pretty wives. But no matter how much he has, he always feel like there's something missing. Something he lost way back when he was a kid.

When he's old and dying, he's lying in bed gazing at one of those glass globes that you shake and the snow starts swirling all around, and it reminds him of the snowy day when his mama sent him away and he didn't want to go with the lawyer and he left his sled behind and the sled said ROSEBUD on it.

So he's lying in bed and the globe falls to the floor and he whispers his last word: Rosebud. And I laughed, thinking that my last words might be Mirror Lake.

Thursday, November 26, 1942

We don't even get turkey for Thanksgiving. That's how bad this place is. They gave us baloney.

Saturday, November 28, 1942

Kenny heard that the food in the Block R mess hall was better than ours, so we went over there last night. It was a waste of time. A cold sardine is a cold sardine, no matter how you slice it. We ate fast and got back in time for some canned sausage and canned spinach. "If it ain't in a can, it ain't in the camp."

Tuesday, December 1, 1942

I decided to start my own rumor. There are so many around here that I thought it might be one to fun to have one of my own. I decided Charles would be a good place to start. He believes pretty much anything I tell him. I told him that I had uncovered secret information that each week the administration is going to choose a family that best represents the cooperative spirit of Mirror Lake. That family will be named The Mirror Lake Model Resident Family of the Month and will be rewarded with a special dinner in their honor, where they will be allowed to eat with the project director and pose for a picture in the camp newspaper.

Charles, just as I figured, was eager to hear how he could enter. He couldn't wait to get back to the Hamada clan and get them geared up for a run at the prize. It's little things like this that make living in Mirror Lake a real dream come true.

Friday, December 4, 1942

This morning I heard Mama and Aunt Mitsuko talking in a low whisper. They stopped as soon as they saw me. All I heard was Mama saying "*Kodomo no tame.*"

I'm glad they're doing something for our sakes, but I wish I knew what it was and I wish they would do it soon.

Thursday, December 10, 1942

There are rumors that there has been a riot in one of the other camps, although no one is sure which one. I didn't even know there *were* other camps.

They say that truckloads of soldiers have been called in and are patrolling the streets with tommy guns. Supposedly, hundreds of people are dead because of the teargas grenades. They say the trouble began because this week is the first anniversary of Pearl Harbor.

Of course, there's no mention about this in the *Free Press*.

Friday, December 11, 1942

Mr. Tashima somehow managed to get his hands on a jar of Ovaltine. It's a miracle. It was the first good thing I've had to eat since I got here. We can't get any milk, so me, Naomi, and Jimmy just stuck in our spoons and ate it. I'd rather have milk but they only let babies have milk. There isn't enough for everyone.

Jimmy didn't look too happy so I asked him if something was wrong. At first he just shook his head, but I could tell that he really did want to tell me. I said I thought we were best friends, and that best friends didn't have secrets.

Jimmy said that some of the other kids said that the FBI wasn't going to let Santa Claus land in Mirror Lake this Christmas. He asked me if that was true. I must admit he had me stumped. I told him I didn't think the FBI was powerful enough to tell Santa Claus where he could or couldn't land but — and I emphasized that it was a big *but* — since we moved out here so suddenly, maybe Santa will have trouble finding us. "We'll just have to wait and see," I said. I hate when grown-ups say "we'll just have to wait and see." Now here I was talking just like them. But it looked like Jimmy believed me.

Monday, December 21, 1942

Mama and Aunt Mitsuko are cleaning the apartment from top to bottom, so it will look nice for Christmas and New Year's. Mama's making *mochi* and buckwheat noodles in chicken broth. I told her I didn't know she could actually make *mochi*, because we always went to Japantown to buy it. But that's kind of out of the question this year.

Mrs. Watanabe and the baby are coming, too. Mrs. Watanabe isn't sick anymore.

Thursday, December 24, 1942

This is the first Christmas we're not going to have a tree. If Papa were here he'd really be happy about that. He hated driving all the way to Livingston's to get a tree. He didn't care much for stuff like that: trees, holidays. "It's how you live every day that counts, Ben." That's what he would say.

I try not to think about Papa, but sometimes I'm not too successful. I wonder if Mama and Naomi think about him. I think they do, but no one ever says anything. I would like to ask Mama but I'm afraid. Not afraid of what she might do or say, but afraid it might upset her. I'm even afraid to ask Naomi.

Last Christmas was the first Christmas without Papa. This will be the second.

Friday, December 25, 1942

Charles cornered me in Wreck Hall and pleaded with me to play Ping-Pong with him, so we played a couple of games. Actually, I should say I played a couple of games because I'm not sure what Charles was doing.

First of all, he's forever blowing his nose into that disgusting handkerchief he's got stuffed into his back pocket. And when he's not sneezing, he's talking. He can't stop even when he's playing. It's like he's afraid he'll die if he stops talking. I told him that if he would be quiet for a second and concentrate on what he's doing, he would score more points. That turned out to be entirely wrong. Even when he did shut up, he hit every shot into the net or about a thousand feet off the table.

Tuesday, December 29, 1942

When it's quiet at night I can hear Mama's slow, even breathing. She doesn't stir, but I don't know if that's because she's sleeping or just lying still, awake.

Friday, January 1, 1943

Well, I never thought I would miss all that Japanese stuff Mama used to make to celebrate New Year's Day: the bamboo shoots and taro, whole red snapper, raw tuna, fried soybean cake. All that stuff. But I sure do miss it now.

Mr. Tashima tried to make it a special day, though. He put a bamboo reed over the front door. He said it stood for family unity. "A strong family," he said, "will bend but never break." That's just what Papa said the night they took him away.

Mr. Tashima had some *sake*, which one of the block managers somehow got hold of. He poured everyone a little, even me and Naomi, so we could all drink a toast together. "To better times than these," Mr. Tashima said. He always tries to look on the sunnier side of things, but even he's getting worn down here.

Friday, January 8, 1943

A letter from Papa.

A lot of the words were crossed out by someone, so it was kind of hard to read. But the important thing is that he's okay. His interviews with the authorities are over, and he'll be arriving Monday on the ten o'clock train.

Mama and Naomi have already decided what they're wearing, and Naomi has painted a beautiful WELCOME HOME, PAPA sign. Mr. Tashima's going to hang it up outside just as soon as it dries.

Monday, January 11, 1943

Papa came home today. But it was not like I thought it would be. I ran up to him and gave him a big hug, but he didn't give me a big hug back. It was like he wasn't sure who I was. He didn't look like he knew Mama or Naomi either.

Mama tried not to show how shaken she was but it was impossible. Everyone's disappointment was too great. I didn't cry, though.

When we got back to the apartment, Papa didn't even notice Naomi's sign, which was unusual. Papa always made such a big deal over everything Naomi did — I mean *everything*. It used to get me so mad. And now, he didn't even see the sign. Just walked past it and put his bag down on the bed and said he was tired from the trip and would like to take a nap.

Mr. Tashima said we should give Papa time to recover from his ordeal. I understand that, but he didn't even look like he was glad to see us.

Wednesday, January 13, 1943

We got another package from Mr. Mills today. He sent us soap and shower caps because he heard that we needed things like that, and almond cookies for me and Naomi because "soap isn't much fun."

Someone had opened the package and looked through everything. They even ate some of the cookies.

Monday, January 18, 1943

The sewers must have gotten clogged up again. They keep digging up the pipes, fixing them, and burying them back in the ground. Then, two weeks later, they have to dig them back up again. It stinks here — in more ways than one.

Saturday, January 23, 1943

Let's just say this hasn't been the best birthday of my life. Naomi gave me a drawing which looks exactly like me, and Mama made me *soba* noodles. Mr. Tashima made me a bright orange kite. It's a real beauty. Maybe I should say, *was* a real beauty.

The thing is, we took it out for a test run and were doing all right until, for no reason at all, it came down in a sudden nosedive, getting ripped to shreds when it hit the barbed wire on top of the electric fence. When the wind finally blew it off, Naomi was the only one brave enough to go get it. When she brought back what was left, Jimmy said, "Bye, bye, birthday present." He got that right.

Monday, January 25, 1943

Papa has been sick. He hasn't gotten out of bed since Thursday. I brought him some soup from the mess hall. They let you do that if someone is so sick they can't come themselves. You don't even have to get down on your knees and beg.

He was able to sit up, but I had to feed him. Mama just sat at the table and watched. It's hard to know what she's thinking.

Wednesday, January 27, 1942

Papa is still too weak to get out of bed.

Saturday, January 30, 1943

I finally wrote Robbie a letter. I wanted to tell him about Mr. Watanabe and a lot of the other things that are going on around here, but I was afraid I would get into trouble.

Instead I just told him how much I hated school, about losing the championship, and about how Papa is back with us now. I didn't say anything about how odd he's acting, though. I didn't tell him that he still has that same "window pane" look on his face. Naomi calls it "window pane" because it's like he's looking right through you. She did a drawing of him sitting on the bench and it looks real sad.

Sometimes I don't even think of him as Papa. He looks like my papa, but he doesn't act like him. The papa I knew was the one the FBI took away with them that night back home in San Francisco. I don't know what happened in that place in Montana, but they took the life out of my papa and left me just the shell.

The only thing Papa does do is play *Go*. If it wasn't for that stupid board game he would just spend all day sitting on the bench outside the apartment, staring. He doesn't even read anymore, and he used to read all the time. I can't hardly picture Papa without a book or a newspaper in front of him. I used to love it when he would read

the paper on Sunday mornings. He would get so mad at all the crazy things that were going on in the world, and make Mama listen while he read out loud. Mama acted like she didn't want to hear about it, but she liked listening to Papa. Now he doesn't read anything to her.

Mama and me took him to the library last week, after school. Of course Charles Hamada was already there when we walked in. Charles got up immediately and offered Papa his seat like there weren't about a zillion other places for him to sit. He took Papa's hand and pumped it up and down like it was an oil well. He told Papa it was really good to see him, like they had been best friends their whole lives.

Papa just smiled and shook his head, which is how he reacts to pretty much everything now. He just sat there while Charles told Mama what a giant brain he was and I tried not to puke. It was pretty boring. Finally even Papa had enough of Charles, and said he wanted to play *Go*.

The only other thing Papa does is listen to the radio so he can hear how the war is going. I watch sometimes when he listens, and I wonder who he's rooting for.

Wednesday, February 3, 1943

This is the happiest I've ever seen Mr. Tashima. Aunt Mitsuko came back from the post office with a letter from his wife. *They are all right.* Both of them are staying with Mr. Tashima's brother and his family in Hiroshima.

Thursday, February 4, 1943

Naomi taught Mama and Aunt Mitsuko to play cat's cradle. They play while Naomi draws and corrects them when they get all tangled up.

Naomi's working on a sketch of the guard tower. As long as she has her pencils and drawing paper she's happy.

Friday, February 5, 1943

And now, the winner in the LET'S MAKE BELIEVE WE'RE IN THE REAL WORLD AND NOT IN THE MIDDLE OF NOWHERE CONTEST: THE MIRROR LAKE SCHOOL ADMINISTRATION.

These folks are actually going to have a full-scale GRADUATION CEREMONY — complete with caps and gowns that a nearby high school is lending to them.

There are going to be real-live boring speeches, bogus awards, and worthless diplomas just like Caucasian kids get. Seventy-five lucky lads and lassies are going to have the honor of being Mirror Lake High's First Graduating Class. Word is that they're going to be given class handcuffs instead of class rings.

Tuesday, February 9, 1943

There was an emergency meeting in Wreck Hall yesterday. The MPs drove around in trucks all morning announcing through their bullhorns that ATTENDANCE IS MANDATORY and THERE WILL BE NO EXCEPTIONS.

Josselit gave one of his fabulous speeches while his assistants handed out these questionnaires they want us to answer. I don't have to, though, because I'm not seventeen yet. Lucky me. The questionnaires were sent all the way from Washington, so it's a big deal. Everyone has to fill them out.

That wasn't the only big news. This was a real red-letter day for Josselit. Not one, but two big announcements.

The second announcement was that the U.S. military was accepting volunteers for an all Japanese-American combat squad. He looked real pleased with himself, like he just announced that the mess hall menu would be changed to prime rib and lobster. I think he thought people were going to rush to the stage and fling themselves at his feet crying, "Take me, take me." Instead, the announcement was met with a deafening silence. You could tell he was unhappy. But that wasn't the end.

He introduced a five-man recruiting team that came up on stage and sat on these folding chairs behind him. Obviously this whole thing was a setup. He said, "these gallant men" would be happy to answer any questions or talk to anyone who wanted to sign up.

Although everyone was talking to everyone else, nobody had the nerve to stand up and ask a question. But after a minute or so a man in the back yelled, "I have a question." The man wanted to know why the Japanese-Americans were being segregated from the rest of the military. Why they weren't being treated the same as other Americans?

One of the soldiers on the recruiting team got up and walked right to the edge of the stage. He was Japanese and looked like a pretty serious guy. All of a sudden it got real, real quiet. The soldier had one of those calm voices. The kind where you know the guy would never panic, no matter what. The kind of guy you want next to you in your foxhole. The soldier said that if we were just mixed in with the millions of other men in uniform, no one would know how brave and loyal Japanese-Americans really are. By forming a separate fighting unit, we can show that we, too, are willing to risk our lives to defend our country.

He looked pretty pleased with himself. Like he was sure this would put an end to any further discussion. But the man in the back wasn't done yet. He almost shouted and his voice was filled with emotion. Why should he risk his life for a country that had made it plain he wasn't wanted? A country that had arrested him without cause, put him behind barbed wire without evidence, and kept him there without a trial? He thought the government of the United States considered us all potential spies and traitors. What changed their minds? Why do they now want us to get killed just like Caucasian boys??

I had to admit that the soldier had a better answer than I thought he would. He said that America would win the war and he warned everyone to make no mistake about that. Japanese-Americans, he said, better start thinking about their lives *after* the war. And an all Japanese-American combat squad was the best way to show that we are Americans first, last, and always.

Tuesday, february 16, 1943

The questionnaire is causing even more problems than the recruiting for the Japanese-American combat squad. No one is sure what the questionnaire is going to be used for. And, since no one trusts the administration, the rumors just keep flying.

Josselit has suspended all activities this past week so everyone can have time to answer all the questions. Of course, this has given everyone plenty of time to argue and get upset and frightened.

One problem is that the questionnaire is called AN APPLICATION FOR LEAVE CLEARANCE. No one knows what LEAVE CLEARANCE means. Some think it means we're going home soon. But even that doesn't make everyone happy. Some of the ladies and old folks don't want to go home. They say life is easier here. They don't have to cook and clean. The administration takes care of everything, so why go home? Besides, they're afraid that if they go home they might be killed. I must admit that being killed would be a big drawback.

Some say it's a trick. That they called it AN APPLICATION FOR LEAVE CLEARANCE so that we would think it was so we could go home, but no one's really sure what it's for.

Two questions are causing the most trouble:

27. Are you willing to serve in the
Armed Forces of the United States on
Combat Duty, wherever ordered?

28. Will you swear unqualified allegiance
to the United States of America and
faithfully defend the United States from
any or all attack by foreign or domestic
forces, and foreswear any form of
allegiance to the Japanese emperor,
or any other foreign government, power
or organization?

No one knows what will happen if you answer yes to both questions or what will happen if you answer no. Some say that if you answer yes you'll be sent home, and that if you answer no you'll be sent to a special camp just for people who said no. That way the government can keep a close eye on all the troublemakers. Naomi's even heard that if you answer no, you'll be sent to Japan.

Kenny's father and mother are going to answer no to both questions so they can go back to Japan. Kenny's father says that Japan is the only place they'll be safe. Kenny thinks they're crazy. Japan is going to lose the war, and then where will they be? He doesn't want to go to Japan. He's never even been to Japan.

There have been secret meetings every night this week on every block. Mr. Tashima is very busy. He looks tired and worried.

I heard Mama talking to him about the two questions. Mr. Tashima told Mama the best thing to do is answer YES to both. I am glad she is listening to his advice. I think most of the people here would just like to stay out of trouble. They don't want to say YES-YES and they don't want to say NO-NO. They don't know what to do.

I'm thinking of organizing a MAYBE-MAYBE group.

Epilogue

◈

Mrs. Tashima and her daughter Midori were killed on August 6, 1945, when the Americans dropped the atom bomb on Hiroshima.

Mr. Tashima and Aunt Mitsuko did not return to San Francisco, relocating instead to Chicago. Mr. Tashima prospered as a much sought-after furniture maker, his business growing so large that he needed Aunt Mitsuko to handle the administrative end.

Jimmy, who became known as "JT," grew up to be an even better carpenter than his father, joining him in business in 1956. At that point the name was changed to TASHIMA AND SON, FURNITURE MAKERS.

Mike Masuda was shot and killed by California State Troopers during an attempted bank robbery.

The Uchida family returned to San Francisco to find that the house they had lived in all their lives had been burned to the ground. The authorities believed the fire to have been "of suspicious origin," but no one was ever brought to justice.

Mr. Mills took them all in, but Mr. Uchida's health deteriorated rapidly and he died in 1945. Mrs. Uchida never remarried.

Two years later, Naomi moved to Denver, Colorado, where her (Caucasian) fiancé taught high school. They had three children, all boys.

Ben Uchida and Robbie Bradley remained best friends their whole lives. Robbie married Veronica Brooks the same year he and Ben opened their first R AND B SPORTING GOODS store. ("We've Got The Goods" was their slogan.)

Robbie and Veronica had two children, a boy and a girl. Ben never married, but became close to Robbie's kids while frequently visiting his nephews in Denver. He was known, and much loved by all, as Uncle Ben.

Life in America
in 1942

Historical Note

When Japan attacked Pearl Harbor on December 7, 1941, it led the American Government to commit an act that is remembered as one of the most embarrassing mistakes in our history. On February 19, 1942, fearing that Japanese Americans were a danger to the United States, President Franklin Delano Roosevelt signed Executive Order 9066, which authorized the exclusion of people from any area for military necessity. This order was the excuse for the mass evacuation and incarceration of 120,000 Japanese Americans, seventy percent of whom were citizens by birth, having been born on American soil.

The prisoners were forced to sell their businesses, properties, and possessions at huge losses, and could take with them only what they could carry. The families were given tags with an identifying number to be worn on coat lapels and attached to suitcases. They were herded onto buses and trains for destinations unknown to them. In violation of the Constitution and without due process of law, these American citizens were held in ten concentration camps, as Roosevelt called them, in the most desolate areas of California, Arizona, Utah, Idaho, Arkansas, Colorado, and Wyoming. Interestingly enough, even though the U.S. was also at war with Germany and Italy, no German or Italian enemy aliens or German or Italian Americans were subjected to these Exclusion Orders — only Japanese aliens and non-aliens.

Why would the U.S. government fear a group of people so much that it would send them to a place where they were held behind barbed wire, with armed guards in lookout towers watching their every move? The United States government had a history of discrimination against Asians that began in the mid-1800s. They were subjected to more discriminatory racist laws than most other immigrant groups in the United States.

During the California gold rush years of 1851–52, the news of a "Gold Mountain" swelled the wave of immigration from China. Despite the foreign miners' tax, passed in 1850 to discourage immigration to the gold mines, twenty-five percent of the miners were Chinese. A much larger number of Chinese laborers helped build the transcontinental railroad. They were assigned the most difficult, dangerous jobs on the railroad.

The anti-Asian discrimination that would lead to the Japanese being interned was already beginning. And the government supported it. Local, state, and federal laws were instituted against the Chinese. In 1850, California State Constitution Article 19 granted cities the authority to expel or segregate Chinese inhabitants. They couldn't become naturalized citizens, testify against whites in court, engage in professions or businesses which required licenses, intermarry with whites, or attend local schools.

The 1870s were a particularly violent decade for the Chinese. Driven from their homes and settlements, many were murdered and lynched, their possessions looted and burned. Later, the U.S. Congress passed the Chinese Exclusion Act of 1882, which stopped Chinese immigration for a ten-year period and denied future citizenship to Chinese already in the country. Eventually, Congress passed additional laws banning immigration on a permanent basis. Without the Chinese immigrants, agricultural concerns in the Western states were left without a source of cheap labor. They sought help from Japan. In 1900, there were 61,000 Japanese laborers in the western United States and the Territory of Hawaii. They were subjected to the same discriminatory laws as the Chinese. Nevertheless, they established roots in this country. Unlike the Chinese, they had families and children who were American citizens by birth.

In 1907, however, under pressure from the United States, the Japanese government agreed to limit emigration to the United States in what was called the Gentleman's Agreement. Japanese were further insulted when the First Alien Land Law was passed in California, prohibiting all foreigners —"aliens ineligible for citizenship"— from owning land. They could lease property for only a limited amount of time. This law was directed primarily at the Japanese and Chinese, who couldn't become naturalized citizens.

Despite the fact that they couldn't own property, the majority of the Japanese were farmers. Over time, they used their skills and their ability to lease property to become an significant part of the agricultural economy. They cultivated areas that the white farmers had neglected. In Southern California, the production of vegetables and fruits was dominated by Japanese farmers. While the average value per acre in the Western Coastal states was $37.94, the average value per acre on a Japanese farm was $279.96. These vastly different values suggest just how successful the Japanese were as farmers.

After World War I, rising anti-Japanese sentiment on the West Coast led to the creation of such groups as the Oriental Exclusion League. Their basic demands included banning all Japanese immigration, maintaining the law denying naturalization to Asians, and denying citizenship to American-born Asians. They also asked that the Gentleman's Agreement, which had allowed a certain number of Japanese to immigrate to the U.S., be cancelled. The

Immigration Act of 1924, also known as the National Origins Act or, more precisely, the Asian Exclusion Act, was passed by the U.S. Congress. This act established quotas that stopped all Asian immigration to the United States from 1924 to 1952, when the McCarran-Walter Immigration and Naturalization Act specified quotas for all countries, including Asian ones. The McCarran-Walter Act also allowed *Issei*, Japanese who were the first generation to live in America, to become naturalized citizens.

The growing tension on the international scene in the 1930s culminated in the attack on Pearl Harbor. Addressing Congress immediately after the bombing, President Roosevelt called it the "Day of Infamy." Less than four months later, notices of the Civilian Exclusion Order that would send the Japanese to the internment camps began to appear.

Approximately one hundred Americans of Japanese descent challenged the evacuation and incarceration orders; four took their cases to the Supreme Court. The Supreme Court upheld Executive Order 9066, concluding that during a wartime emergency, any group of people can be incarcerated without due process of law. Later, in 1944, Associate Justice Frank Murphy of the U.S. Supreme Court called the order the "legalization of racism."

The leading advocates of mass exclusion and incarceration were General John L. DeWitt and his staff at the Western Defense Command. They accused Japanese Americans of sabotage and espionage. Prior to this, in 1941, when relations between the U.S. and Japan were threatened by rumors of war, President Roosevelt had sent Curtis B. Munson, a special representative to the State Department, to investigate the activities of Japanese-American communities in Hawaii and on the West Coast. The Munson Report, submitted in November of that year, certified that there was a remarkable and extraordinary degree of loyalty among Japanese Americans. This confirmed similar studies that were performed by the F.B.I. and Naval Intelligence.

In spite of the gross injustices perpetrated against them, thousands of Japanese Americans from the internment camps and Hawaii volunteered to serve in the U.S. Armed Forces. They formed the 442nd Regimental Combat Team, which became the most decorated fighting unit of its size in American military history. Japanese-American soldiers were the first to liberate the Jewish inmates in Dachau Concentration Camp on April 14, 1944, but this news was suppressed by the U.S. Government. The families of some of these soldiers were being held in camps very similar to Dachau back in the U.S. In addition, 6,000 Japanese-American soldiers served in the Military Intelligence Service in the South Pacific. According to a ranking intelligence officer under General Douglas

MacArthur, their contributions shortened the Pacific War by two years, saving two million lives. During World War II, not even a single case of subversive activity was found to be committed by a Japanese American.

On February 19, 1976, President Gerald R. Ford rescinded the thirty-four-year-old Executive Order 9066 and stated, "An honest reckoning must include a recognition of our national mistakes as well as our national achievements. Learning from our mistakes is not pleasant, but as a great philosopher once admonished, we must do so if we want to avoid repeating them."

President Ronald Reagan signed the Civil Liberties Act of 1988, which recommended an official U.S. Government apology and a $20,000 restitution to each of the approximately 60,000 internees still living. In his speech after signing the legislation, Reagan paid tribute to a Japanese-American soldier who had died in battle for his country, saying, "Blood that has soaked into the sands of a beach is all of one color. America stands unique in the world, the only country not founded on race, but on a way — an ideal. Not in spite of, but because of our polyglot background, we have had all the strength in the world. That is the American way."

INSTRUCTIONS
TO ALL PERSONS OF
JAPANESE
ANCESTRY
Living in the Following Area:

All of that portion of the City of Los Angeles, State of California, within that boundary beginning at the point at which North Figueroa Street meets a line following the middle of the Los Angeles River; thence southerly and following the said line to East First Street; thence westerly on East First Street to Alameda Street; thence southerly on Alameda Street to East Third Street; thence northwesterly on East Third Street to Main Street; thence northerly on Main Street to First Street; thence northwesterly on First Street to Figueroa Street; thence northeasterly on Figueroa Street to the point of beginning.

Pursuant to the provisions of Civilian Exclusion Order No. 33, this Headquarters, dated May 3, 1942, all persons of Japanese ancestry, both alien and non-alien, will be evacuated from the above area by 12 o'clock noon, P. W. T., Saturday, May 9, 1942.

No Japanese person living in the above area will be permitted to change residence after 12 o'clock noon, P. W. T., Sunday, May 3, 1942, without obtaining special permission from the representative of the Commanding General, Southern California Sector, at the Civil Control Station located at:

Japanese Union Church,
120 North San Pedro Street,
Los Angeles, California.

Such permits will only be granted for the purpose of uniting members of a family, or in cases of grave emergency.

The Civil Control Station is equipped to assist the Japanese population affected by this evacuation in the following ways:

1. Give advice and instructions on the evacuation.
2. Provide services with respect to the management, leasing, sale, storage or other disposition of most kinds of property, such as real estate, business and professional equipment, household goods, boats, automobiles and livestock.
3. Provide temporary residence elsewhere for all Japanese in family groups.
4. Transport persons and a limited amount of clothing and equipment to their new residence.

The Following Instructions Must Be Observed:

1. A responsible member of each family, preferably the head of the family, or the person in whose name most of the property is held, and each individual living alone, will report to the Civil Control Station to receive further instructions. This must be done between 8:00 A. M. and 5:00 P. M. on Monday, May 4, 1942, or between 8:00 A. M. and 5:00 P. M. on Tuesday, May 5, 1942.
2. Evacuees must carry with them on departure for the Assembly Center, the following property:
   (a) Bedding and linens (no mattress) for each member of the family;
   (b) Toilet articles for each member of the family;
   (c) Extra clothing for each member of the family;
   (d) Sufficient knives, forks, spoons, plates, bowls and cups for each member of the family;
   (e) Essential personal effects for each member of the family.

All items carried will be securely packaged, tied and plainly marked with the name of the owner and numbered in accordance with instructions obtained at the Civil Control Station. The size and number of packages is limited to that which can be carried by the individual or family group.

3. No pets of any kind will be permitted.
4. No personal items and no household goods will be shipped to the Assembly Center.
5. The United States Government through its agencies will provide for the storage, at the sole risk of the owner, of the more substantial household items, such as iceboxes, washing machines, pianos and other heavy furniture. Cooking utensils and other small items will be accepted for storage if crated, packed and plainly marked with the name and address of the owner. Only one name and address will be used by a given family.
6. Each family, and individual living alone, will be furnished transportation to the Assembly Center or will be authorized to travel by private automobile in a supervised group. All instructions pertaining to the movement will be obtained at the Civil Control Station.

**Go to the Civil Control Station between the hours of 8:00 A. M. and 5:00 P. M.,
Monday, May 4, 1942, or between the hours of 8:00 A. M. and 5:00 P. M.,
Tuesday, May 5, 1942, to receive further instructions.**

J. L. DeWITT
Lieutenant General, U. S. Army
Commanding

Fearing that they were a danger to America, on February 19, 1942, President Roosevelt signed Executive Order 9066, ordering all people of Japanese ancestry—even if they were American citizens—evacuated from the West Coast. The evacuation took place in two stages: first, into temporary assembly centers, such as the Santa Anita Racetrack; second, into a permanent camp such as Manzanar, California, or Topaz, Utah.

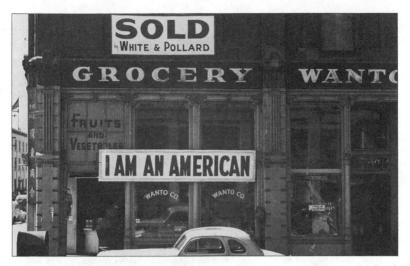

Following rules set forth in Executive Order 9066, this store in San Francisco was closed. The owner, a Japanese American, hung the I AM AN AMERICAN sign on the storefront on December 8, 1941, the day after Pearl Harbor.

One member of each family was asked to report to the Civil Control Station, where they would receive instructions on the evacuation, assistance with property storage and sale, and an identification number. Tags with the identification number were worn on coat lapels and attached to suitcases for the trip to the assembly centers and permanent camps. Families could bring with them only what they could carry.

143

When packing for their journey to the camps, the detainees were instructed to bring bedding and linens, toilet articles, extra clothing, eating utensils and dishes, and essential personal effects for each member of the family. On arriving at the camps, families had to search through huge piles of luggage for their belongings.

At certain times between June 1941 to November 1945, the population of Manzanar grew to more than 10,000 prisoners. The barracks were constructed of wooden frames with tar paper roofs and plywood walls. According to army regulations, this type of housing was suitable only for combat-trained soldiers on a temporary basis, but at Manzanar, men, women, and children lived there for up to three and a half years.

Each barrack was divided into apartments. On average, eight people were assigned to one 20-by-25-foot apartment. Although the furnishings provided were sparse—iron cots, bags to be filled with straw for mattresses, and army blankets—many families used scrap lumber to build furniture, which made for a more pleasant environment.

Despite the long lines, the mess halls were a center of family life. Here, old and young gather around a table for a meal.

The Topaz Times, top, *was the newspaper for the internment camp located at Topaz, Utah. The newspaper staff was made up of camp prisoners, some of whom are shown preparing an edition for delivery,* bottom. *Newspapers, which were censored by camp administrators, included camp, national, and international news; editorials; and advertisements.*

Baseball was a popular sport with many of the interned. Organized teams and leagues were formed at camps such as Tule Lake (shown here) and Manzanar. At Manzanar, an "all-star" baseball game was played as part of the July 4, 1942, celebration, which also included band concerts, picnics, and a beauty contest. Fireworks were planned in the spirit of Independence Day, but they were canceled, probably for security reasons.

The Japanese had a strong commitment to education, which continued in the camps. Classes were taught by both Caucasian and Japanese instructors, but the Japanese received a much lower salary. Although the schools lacked supplies, they eventually became fully accredited, meeting or exceeding state standards for education.

147

Manzanar was surrounded by guard towers equipped with searchlights and machine guns. Several residents of the camps were killed by sentries for allegedly trying to escape.

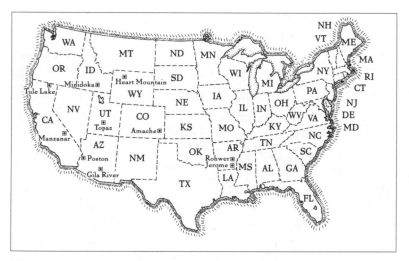

This map of the United States shows the locations of the ten permanent relocation centers that held detainees from March 1942 until their closings in 1945 and 1946.

TOYO MIYATAKE, 1895 – 1979

Toyo Miyatake photographed the boy in the cover portrait while they were imprisoned in Manzanar, the first of ten internment camps built by the U.S. government to house Japanese Americans during the war.

Toyo Miyatake, born in Zentsuji, Japan, was the second son of a Buddhist monk. When he was fourteen, his family immigrated to Los Angeles, California, where they ran a confectionary shop. Toyo Miyatake became a professional photographer, studying with Edward Weston, a significant figure in the history of American photography.

For the duration of World War II, Miyatake and his family lived in Manzanar. Determined to keep a photographic diary of his life there, Miyatake smuggled a camera lens and film holder into the camp. With these basic components, he built a crude wooden camera and proceeded to create a detailed, comprehensive photographic record of life in Manzanar. When the camp's director, Ralph Merritt, discovered that Miyatake was disobeying the law, rather than having him arrested, he allowed Miyatake to send for the rest of his equipment. In later years, Miyatake would refer to this photographic project as his "historic duty." In fact, he produced the most important visual record of the internment experience, and his images have been used in dozens of publications and featured in television documentaries about the camps.

After the war, Miyatake and his sons reopened their family photo studio in the Little Toyko section of Los Angeles, producing the stylish, evocative portraits that were the Miyatake trademark. Among his more famous subjects were Japanese Crown Prince Akihito, dance pioneer Michio Ito, and author Thomas Mann.

Toyo Miyatake's son, Archie, was inspired by his father's courage and determination to document their life in the Manzanar camp. While imprisoned, Archie learned the art of photography from his father, becoming an accomplished photographer in his own right. His portrait subjects have included the Emperor of Japan, Marilyn Monroe, and Gary Cooper. Currently, Archie Miyatake's main endeavor is the preservation and promotion of the Toyo Miyatake Manzanar Photographic Archive. Its purpose is to educate future generations about this important and tragic moment in American history. Archie Miyatake lives in Montebello, California, with his wife. He has two grown sons.

Norito Takamoto, age nine (left), Bruce Sansui, age twelve (middle), and Masaaki Ooka, age nine (right), were photographed by Toyo Miyatake at Manzanar.

This photograph shows Toyo (left) and Archie (right) Miyatake at the Poston Relocation Center in Arizona. In 1945, right before Manzanar closed, they were given permission to travel to Poston and take photographs of the camp there.

About the Author

BARRY DENENBERG is the author of several critically acclaimed books for young readers, including one book in the My Name Is America series, *The Journal of William Thomas Emerson: A Revolutionary War Patriot*; and two books in the Dear America series, *When Will This Cruel War Be Over?: The Civil War Diary of Emma Simpson*, which was named an NCSS Notable Children's Trade Book in the Field of Social Studies and a YALSA Quick Pick; and *So Far From Home: The Diary of Mary Driscoll, an Irish Mill Girl.* Praised for his meticulous research, Barry Denenberg has written books about diverse times in American history, from the Civil War to Vietnam.

About *The Journal of Ben Uchida*, Denenberg says, "I wanted to write Ben Uchida's story because it is unique. Two-thirds of the 110,000 Japanese Americans imprisoned were American citizens. This makes it the most widespread U.S. government action against its own people in our history.

"Two-thirds were in their early twenties or younger.

Nearly six thousand babies were born in the camps. The internment experience was a family experience. More than in any other event in American history, kids were the central focus of the story.

"It would, I thought, be best to see it through their eyes."

Denenberg's nonfiction works include *An American Hero: The True Story of Charles A. Lindbergh,* which was named an ALA Best Book for Young Adults and a New York Public Library Book for the Teen Age; and *Voices from Vietnam,* an ALA Best Book for Young Adults, a *Booklist* Editors' Choice, and a New York Public Library Book for the Teen Age. He lives with his wife and their daughter in Westchester County, New York.

This book is dedicated to:

Megan	Annie	Alexandra	Sarah
Katie	Bridgett	Eric	Monica
Jasmyn	Krista	Brianna	Tommy
Beth	Hillari	Shawn	Sylvia
April	Shannon	Phillip	Sabrina
Henry	Elizabeth	Peter	Craig
Nicole	Edward	Don	Tory
Kristen	Tracy	Storrs	Bobbi
Freddy	Allison	Jake	Alyson
Andrea	Melissa	Kassy	Keri
Ashley	Jade	McKenna	Tara
Kimberly	Erica	Molly	Laurel
Valerie	Alyssa	Jenna	Aryn
Bette	Kelsey	Christine	Rhonda
Mary	Erin	Brodie	Jessica
Michele	Rachel	Sara	Lauren
Julia	Jamie	Robbyn	Courtney
Teddy	Brittany	Jennifer	Leah
Amber	Samantha	Kate	Andrew
Amanda	Holly	Kayla	Michelle
Nadia	Kniccoa	Brooke	Rosemary
Amy	Victoria		

And all those who took the time to write.

Acknowledgments

◆

The author would like to thank Amy Griffin for her sensitive editorial work and Chris Kearin and his fellow "book people" for their help.

◆

Grateful acknowledgment is made for permission to reprint the following:
Cover portrait: Photograph of Bruce Sansui, Miyatake Collection.
Cover background: Barbed wire, National Japanese American Historical Society.

Interior illustrations by Jennifer Presant.
Foldout photograph, Miyatake Collection.

Page 143 (top): Closed store, California Historical Society.
Page 143 (bottom): Photograph of family by Dorothea Lange, National Archives.
Page 144 (top): Luggage, National Archives, National Japanese American Historical Society.
Page 144 (bottom): Barracks at Manzanar, Miyatake Collection.
Page 145 (top): Apartment, National Archives, National Japanese American Historical Society.
Page 145 (bottom): Mess hall, AP/Wide World.
Page 146 (top): *Topaz Times*, Manuscripts Division, J. Willard Marriott Library, University of Utah.
Page 146 (bottom): Workers at the *Topaz Times*, Photograph Archives, Utah State Historical Society.
Page 147 (top): Baseball game, Manuscripts Division, J. Willard Marriott Library, University of Utah.
Page 147 (bottom): Classroom, Photograph Archives, Utah State Historical Society.
Page 148 (top): Sign, War Relocation Authority.
Page 148 (bottom): Map by Heather Saunders.
Page 151 (top): Boys at Manzanar, Miyatake Collection.
Page 151 (bottom): Toyo and Archie Miyatake, Miyatake Collection.

Other books in the My Name Is America series

The Journal of William Thomas Emerson
A Revolutionary War Patriot
by Barry Denenberg

The Journal of James Edmond Pease
A Civil War Union Soldier
by Jim Murphy

The Journal of Joshua Loper
A Black Cowboy
by Walter Dean Myers

The Journal of Scott Pendleton Collins
A World War II Soldier
by Walter Dean Myers

The Journal of Sean Sullivan
A Transcontinental Railroad Worker
by William Durbin

Copyright © 1999 by Barry Denenberg

◈

All rights reserved. Published by Scholastic Inc.
SCHOLASTIC, MY NAME IS AMERICA and associated logos are trademarks and/or registered trademarks of Scholastic Inc.

Library of Congress Cataloging-in-Publication Data

Denenberg, Barry
The journal of Ben Uchida, citizen 13559, Mirror Lake internment camp /
by Barry Denenberg. — 1st ed.
p.   cm. — (My name is America)
Summary: Twelve-year-old Ben Uchida keeps a journal of his experiences as a
prisoner in a Japanese internment camp in Mirror Lake, California, during
World War II.

ISBN 0-590-48531-8

[1. Japanese Americans — Evacuation and relocation, 1942–1945 — Juvenile
fiction. [1. Japanese Americans — Evacuation and relocation, 1942–1945 —
Fiction.   2. World War, 1939–1945 — United States — Fiction.
3. Diaries — Fiction.]   I. Title.   II. Series.
PZ7.D4135Jn   1999
[Fic] — dc21   98-40956
CIP   AC

10   9   8   7   6   5   4   3   2   1   9/9   0/0   01   02   03

The display type was set in Capone Medium Condensed.
The text type was set in Berling Roman.
Book design by Elizabeth B. Parisi
Photo research by Zoe Moffitt and Pamela Heller

Printed in the U.S.A.   23
First edition, September 1999

◈

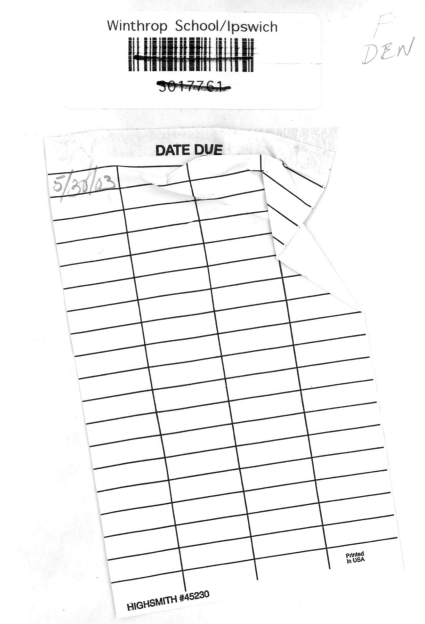